Dear Reader:

I am delighted to present to you *Playing in the Dark*, the third in a series by David Rivera, Jr. For those of you who have followed the author's first novels, *Harlem's Dragon* and *The Street Sweeper*, you know that he is a talented writer who blends suspense with erotica. On the cover of *The Street Sweeper* is the incredibly sexy model from movies like Tyler Perry's *Madea's Family Reunion*. Yes, he was the stripper dressed as a police officer. He is hot and so is the author of this book: David Rivera, Jr.

Rivera has penned yet another powerful tale involving Chemah, a police detective of both African-American and Latino descent, who is not only all about doing his job right but also doing his women right.

If you haven't read *Harlem's Dragon* and *The Street Sweeper*, you will love them as well as *Playing in the Dark*. The titles in the trilogy are all written without the need to read in a particular sequence, however, I would encourage you to read them all.

Thank you for supporting Mr. Rivera's efforts and thank you for supporting one of the dozens of authors published under my imprint, Strebor Books. I try my best to bring you cutting-edge works of literature that will keep your attention and make you think long after you turn the last page.

Now sit back in your favorite chair or, better yet, chill in the bed, and be prepared to be tantalized by yet another great read.

Peace and Many Blessings,

Zane

Publisher
Strebor Books
www.simonsays.com/streborbooks

ALSO BY DAVID RIVERA, JR.

The Street Sweeper

Harlem's Dragon

ZANE PRESENTS

David Rivera, Jr.

Playing in the Dark

THE EMPTINESS THAT LOVE BRINGS...

SBI
STREBOR BOOKS
NEW YORK LONDON TORONTO SYDNEY

Strebor Books
P.O. Box 6505
Largo, MD 20792
http://www.streborbooks.com

ISBN-13 978-1-59309-181-1
ISBN-10 1-59309-181-8
LCCN 2007941390

First Strebor Books trade paperback edition February 2008

Cover design: www.mariondesigns.com

10 9 8 7 6 5 4 3 2 1

Manufactured in the United States of America

For information regarding special discounts for bulk purchases, please contact Simon & Schuster Special Sales at 1-800-456-6798 or business@simonandschuster.com

Dedication

This book is dedicated to my sons, David Austin Rivera III, Chemah Seto Rivera, and Tatsuya Goché Rivera. Each of them has given me pause to reflect on how I can be a better writer, father, and human being. I'm blessed to be able to say that they are as much a part of me as I am a part of them.

Acknowledgments

When I wrote my first book, *Harlem's Dragon,* I never suspected that a second—and now a third—book would come from it. So when I give thanks to Harlem Goju, wherein I first saw the principles that the main character in this series projected through my association with Grandmaster Sam McGee and Master Dwayne McGee, it is only fitting that I bow to them in humble appreciation.

To my writing mentor Zane, thank you for the opportunity to do what I was meant to do and helping me on the path to becomng a better writer. To Charmaine, who never seems to be disturbed when things aren't going exactly right. I am grateful for your patience. To Judith Lee-Sing Rivera who has to be credited with directing the photo shoots for every one of my book covers as well as putting up with the mood swings that writing causes in crazy folks like me, my sincere thanks and apologies. To Rehva Jones, who helped me flush out the story told in this last book through her first edits, it would have been extremely difficult without your help. Thanks to Keith Saunders for doing a marvelous job on the cover. He knows what we went through to get the right model. Shout-out to my sister Sheilla Rivera who is my biggest fan and greatest promoter.

Ultimately, I would like to thank everyone in my life who sings the blues with me in my dark times and those whom I hold close when the sun shines glaringly in my life path.

Peace and Love to you all

"There is only one happiness in life, to love and be loved."

—George Sand

Prayer:

May the evil man be good.
May the good man find peace.
May he who finds peace be free.
And may he who is free make others free.

Chapter 1

GENESIS 19 ?

Bereft wound his way through Sodom's crowded streets. He was enjoying the powerful new body he recently acquired. It belonged to a Kemetan slave trader who strayed too far from the spiritual path of his ancestors. Bereft could only possess and corrupt the wayward, but that was not a problem as he could identify those who were open to him easily enough. He had found this one in a house of the most ill repute. The Kemetan was brutally bending the fallen woman's body to his will and Bereft decided to continue fornicating with the whore when he entered the slave trader. The Kemetan was holding her one leg behind her neck and was convulsing a torrent of semen into her when Bereft entered him. The pain in her face was intoxicating to Bereft. The woman was a worthwhile prize and Bereft would have taken her instead if not for her missing leg and his need for a male body at this time. The woman noticed the change in her temporal lover instantly when she saw the passion in his eyes replaced by malice. Bereft would have gotten pleasure from choking the life from her at that moment, but decided to save her for another time. Maybe tomorrow he would come back and break her other leg off. He would fuck her with it, he thought, as he jumped off of her laughing. The woman scampered across the dirty floor to the farthest corner in the hut. Bereft laughed at her fear, absorbing the power he drew from this human emotion.

Bereft's promise to Lot's daughters was a simple one. He would come back to them in a form other than that of the woman he seduced them with the night before. In return they would allow him to secretly observe their father's consecration rituals for fellowship with God. Bereft was convinced that if he could understand God's relationship to men, specifically why God granted them so much mercy and how Lot received his power from God, he would be able to somehow take the power away, harness it for himself, thereby guaranteeing his control over Sodom.

In this city, where every soul was doomed to be lost, any and all spirits could run rampantly without ever being contested, but that freedom was not enough for Bereft. He wanted the absolute authority that came with sovereignty that came with deification. Bereft was recklessly ambitious, he wanted to be more than king of Sodom. He wanted every soul in Sodom subject to his will. He wanted to be a god—adored and worshipped incessantly. Bereft and his four brothers made a grave wager that had driven all but him from this city thus far. It appeared to be an easy bargain. Each brother had one attempt at separating Lot from God. A failed attempt meant banishment from the city forever. His brothers had tried and all had failed. Bereft was the last to try. His attempt at seducing Lot had to be calculated and precise, lest his try at the halo over Lot's head be as futile as his brothers' had been. If he failed this one time, the wager would be null and his brothers would be allowed to return and the city. Sodom would never be his to rule alone.

Lot's daughters, Shelena and Miriam, were waiting for Bereft behind the small shack where the animals were kept. The girls, who were ages twenty and twenty-one respectively, were no match for Bereft's seductive nature. He winked and smiled at them and they knew him as soon as they met his gaze. His eyes were always the same. They smoldered with malevolence. The icy evil in his eyes had a chilling but hypnotic effect on all who looked into them. Despite Bereft's transformative powers, he could not change his eyes or their sinister gaze.

Shelena and Miriam were old maids by the standards of their tribe. Most considered it a sin that they lived with their father without husbands or children. They felt it was disgraceful that their father had not already married them off. They were more beautiful than any other women in the city and they looked so much alike that everyone thought they were twins. Both had olive skin that held no blemishes, their eyes were green like emeralds in pools of water. Their mouths were full and red, yet they wore no paint on their faces. Each had hair so black and thick that all women who saw them were instantly jealous.

Their father, Lot, left them and their mother on many occasions while he went into the mountains to commune with God. When he was gone for long periods, the girls secretly watched their mother entertain assorted men in their father's bed when she thought they were asleep. She allowed men to put the hard fleshy meat they kept between their legs into the soft wet opening between hers. At first, the exhibitions frightened them, the way she would grunt and scream when the men with the biggest flesh under their robes would ram themselves into her. After a time they came to realize that those were the men their mother favored the most. She enjoyed spending time with them and the girls watched and learned the joys of being with men through their spying.

When Bereft left Shelena and Miriam yesterday, they were in a sweated heap on the floor of the stable behind their home. He had introduced them to his body, which at the time was that of a twenty-five-year-old woman whom he had possessed after watching her fornicate with her husband's best friend. First he plied them with wine, knowing that after their hard work with the animals, it would be enough to erase all of their bewilderment at the responses their bodies would have to the lewd acts to be performed. He teased them both with his fingers, simultaneously entering them with the longest digit of each of his hands as they lay on the hay-strewn floor with their legs opened wide. When he brought them to the edge of ecstasy and they could take it no longer, Bereft bent his head to Shelena's venus and placed the full mouth that was now his against the lips that hid her birth opening. Miriam recognized the look on her sister's face immediately. She had seen that look of rapture on her mother's face quite often. She couldn't wait to have this woman's mouth on her birth opening too. When it was her turn, she thrust her hips into the face of the wanton woman boldly. She spilled such copious amounts of fluid into the woman's mouth that she thought at one point that she might be urinating unwittingly.

Now Bereft came to them as a large, onyx-colored male with the features of the royal family of Egypt plainly upon his visage.

"Do you recognize me, Shelena? Miriam?" he addressed one, then the other.

The two young women spent last night in the corner that they shared in their father's hovel, quietly giggling at the crazy woman's claim of having the ability to change her form to that of a man. They discussed, in hushed tones, the experiences they had sharing their bodies with the woman who called herself Bereft and how she succumbed to their beauty, devoutly worshipping their flesh. They fell asleep in a dilemma of guilty pleasure, vacillating between dread for the acts they committed and desire for another encounter with Bereft.

Now Miriam and Shelena stood still as Bereft came toward them. The sisters were frozen in fear. There was no doubt in either of their minds that the entity in front of them and the being who had seduced them yesterday were one and the same.

Bereft held his hand out to Miriam and she could not stop her feet from going to him. Shelena wanted to run, but she found his eyes latched on to her soul and knew that her will was his. When Miriam reached the spot where Bereft stood, he only slightly touched the top of her head and she dropped immediately to her knees in front of him. The front of his robe was frighteningly extended from his waist and she knew the man flesh beneath the robe was more than she or her sister had ever witnessed while watching their mother's affairs. Bereft grabbed a handful of Miriam's hair and pressed her face into his groin. She felt the length of him press against her face, from the tip of her jaw past the top of her head. He kept her face pressed against him as he pulled his robe over his head with his other hand. The fabric of the tunic was rough, scraping her lips raw as he drew it up slowly over his head, taking care to ensure Miriam could not move away. As the fabric gave way to flesh, Miriam's mouth dropped open in astonishment.

"Oh."

Bereft wasted no time. He saw the chasm of her mouth and thrust forward. Miriam's mouth snapped closed in time to keep from being filled.

"Mmm, mmm," she objected through pressed lips. She looked to her younger sister for help, but only saw Shelena licking her lips in anticipation of her turn.

"Open your mouth, beautiful one." Bereft bent over and whispered to her. "The taste of my flesh will be as delectable to your palate today as it was yesterday. I would much rather you drew the essence of this body willingly, child. I would never force the delights of this body on you or anyone else who wasn't of a mind to receive it," he lied through brilliantly white teeth.

Miriam looked to Shelena again and was convinced through the hunger in her sister's eyes that she should at least try this new experience being offered. Her mouth slowly opened and she closed her eyes, waiting for Bereft to thrust into it.

Moments passed with nothing happening. The girl slowly opened one eye to see why the shaft had not filled her mouth. Bereft was not moving his flesh toward her anymore. Instead, he was now beckoning Shelena to him. Miriam could not fathom how he was doing it, for he had not opened his mouth to speak nor did he extend a hand in invitation, yet she could feel and knew his will as her sister stepped behind Bereft and circled her arms around his waist. Miriam was intrigued to see Shelena behaving so boldly and opened her other eye to witness the hold that she had on Bereft and he had on her.

Shelena grasped the thick ebony shaft of meat that protruded from Bereft's body in her hands as if she were once again wielding the shepherd's staff. She pointed the fat mushroom-shaped end at her sister's mouth. Miriam's mouth opened slowly. Instead of allowing the head to enter her sister's mouth, as it was now so very close to doing, she instead jerked it up and away from her, causing Miriam to lunge forward as it moved just out of reach. Bereft and Shelena laughed at Miriam as she sat up, begging like a bitch waiting for a bone from her master's table. Shelena continued to tease Miriam until both the girls could once again feel Bereft's will. Shelena held the large protuberance in her hands steady and Miriam allowed her mouth to go slack as her head fell forward, allowing Bereft's phallus past her lips and into her throat. Miriam wondered at first how she was managing to sheath all of Bereft's girth without gagging. She knew she must be entranced by his spell. Shelena released Bereft's penis just as the last of it went into her sister's mouth. She then fell to her knees behind him, burying her head and tongue into the dark muskiness of his posterior. Shelena had never committed this act before and briefly could not understand how and why she was engaging in such an act of utter repugnance without so much as flinching. But, she, like her sister, knew that it was the spell that Bereft had cast.

Bereft languished in the meal that he made of himself as the two young women recklessly feasted on him. He stood with his hands on his hips, swollen with arrogance at how his plan was coming to fruition.

He would allow them a few more moments to debase themselves and then he would show them such pleasure in a man's body that they would be enslaved to his will and bring him to their father's sanctum. Once Bereft knew how Lot communed with God, he would know just how to seduce the devout servant, bring him to his knees, and make him pray to and worship him. Lot would be permanently separated from the mercy of God, and the souls of Sodom would subject themselves to Bereft's malevolent rule.

‡‡‡

For the first half hour after Bereft had sent Shelena and Miriam back to their father's house, he allowed himself the luxury of remembering how he had made them orgasm repeatedly, each time begging him for more of what he had promised. He had the foresight to stop before they were totally depleted, sending them back to prepare Lot for his fateful meeting. Bereft was not one to worry, but the girls had now been gone for longer than a while. They were only a stone's throw away at their home, and should be preparing their father to meet him, but if that were the case he would be able to sense them now, and he could not. The only other answer was that they were in the presence of someone so holy that he could unwittingly block Bereft from sensing them. From what he had heard of Lot, that may well be the case.

A full hour passed before Bereft finally admitted to himself that something was wrong. He let his senses wander throughout the city and was thrown from his feet by the omnipotent surge of power that was thrust back at him. It wasn't just any power. It was God's power. For the first time in eons, Bereft was scared.

Bereft ran the fifty yards to Lot's house faster than was humanly possible, knowing that he would find the answer to his fear in the heart of a mere mortal. He crashed through the door to the small hut ready to render an answer from this man of God quickly and maybe even painfully, but he found the place empty but for some furnishings that were made from untreated wood and were badly hewn by their maker.

Bereft could feel the omnipresent power move closer. In one final, desperate attempt to find Shelena and Miriam, he allowed his senses to wander again, this time to the outermost parts of the city. He found them on the outskirts of the city, and they were running for their lives.

"They ought not to have thought that they could run from me," he snarled, as he set off after them.

Bereft ran with the swiftness of one whose body had no limits. He was not afraid to use up all of the life force that this body housed to get to Lot's daughters. Within minutes he was in sight of them. They were only a half league away from him now. He thought to be upon them soon when he realized that those whom he had spied were not Lot's daughters, who were still a full league away. It was Lot and his whore of a wife.

Why were they running?

Lot was a faithful manservant of God. Surely he was not running away from the omnipotent power that Bereft felt like a searing hot wind just behind him. Bereft was now just twenty yards behind them. He could barely understand the words Lot yelled to his wife over the howling wind.

"Don't look back! For the love of God, don't look back at the city!"

This made no sense to Bereft and he looked over his shoulder in fear. What he saw was the city crumbling to dust and angel warriors descending upon it. He had left the city just in time. In a way Lot had saved him. At the sight behind him, Bereft attempted to run yet faster, but the life energy of the body he had stolen was almost depleted. He was only twenty feet away from Lot and his wife when she heard the footsteps behind her and turned to see who followed. She saw Bereft first and then the fallen city before she turned white and instantly hardened into a pillar of salt. Bereft was unable to change direction fast enough and ran right into the pillar of salt that Lot's wife had become. He was knocked senseless for a moment.

Before he could get to his feet again, angel warriors were upon him. Their wings were the cause of the howling winds, and intense heat emanated from their swords of fire. There were too many, and they overtook Bereft. They could not kill him for he was not so easily vanquished. But they smote the body that he inhabited and exposed the oozing filth that was Bereft's soul. The essence of Bereft seeped into the soil. The angel warriors entombed the vile essence by shattering the pillar of salt that Lot's wife had become over the soil that held Bereft's soul. The city of Sodom was transformed into a cavernous crypt marking a brackish burial site of its wicked citizens. The angel warriors were satisfied. Bereft would be held for a time.

Chapter 2

Trouble in a Distant land

Chemah hadn't expected Israel to be as hot as it was. He and Michelle dropped off their luggage at the hotel and went straight to the hospital. They were already an hour late, through no fault of their own. The flight was forced to circle the airport for a full hour due to an earlier bombing by the Hezbollah terrorists that the Israeli government was finding hard to contain.

Chemah's shirt was sticking to his thickly muscled chest and he used his thumb and forefinger to open the buttons of the collar and pull it away from his skin. The woman standing next to him and Michelle on the taxi line in front of the hotel smiled at him and fanned herself with her open hand to show that she sympathized with him. She stared into his gray-tinged green eyes long enough to make Chemah blush. In an attempt to ward off the woman's advances, Chemah took Michelle's hand in his. Michelle, who always thought that Chemah's holding her hand made her appear helpless, snatched her hand away. The woman's smile only became broader as she shrugged and dipped her head into the cab in front of her that had just become available. Chemah, whose skin was usually a healthy tanned complexion, now turned red and hot with embarrassment. He felt the sparse, cool air wafting from the hotel door hit the back of his neck and was glad that he tied his nearly waist-length dreadlocks up.

Chemah looked down at Michelle and could see that she was agitated again. It was a silly cliché, but Michelle was most beautiful when she was angry. Recently he noticed that Michelle showed more of her beauty every day. She wore her hair loose and Chemah smiled as he remembered how much angrier she became when anybody mentioned how very long, straight, and beautiful her hair was. Chemah knew that it was naturally like that. He'd met her whole family during a reunion in the Red Hook projects in Brooklyn a year ago. He was glad to meet Michelle's mother, who looked like he imagined Michelle would look in twenty years. She was still very beautiful. The full hips, large breasts, and freckled face were identical to Michelle's and Mrs. Thomas was the only one in the family other than Michelle who had the beautiful, long, straight hair. Michelle was a professional comedienne, but her whole family made jokes about one another and the one thing they all teased Michelle about was the "Indian influence" in her hair.

Chemah looked down and noticed the sweat that dripped down Michelle's cleavage. He was very tempted to move her hair away from her shoulders to afford himself a better view. Michelle sniffed the air, taking in the residual sulfuric taste of a recent firebombing. The smell shocked her senses, causing her to spit a flurry of profanity.

"What the fuck died around here?" she whispered harshly, turning toward Chemah's chest.

Awakened from his romantic reverie, Chemah took in his surroundings and was immediately on guard.

Chemah would never have brought Michelle to the battle zone that Israel had become if he hadn't been forced. There was a new experimental medical procedure that might give Michelle a chance at getting her eyesight back. Her doctor in New York, Dr. Johanson, was an associate of Dr. Yasmin, the doctor whom they were here to see. He'd been an ophthalmological specialist in New York up until three years ago, when he was compelled to come to Israel to help the cause of his people. Dr. Yasmin recently developed a new retinal replacement procedure as a result of his work with the victims whose eyesight had been compromised by the country's insurgent bombings. Finally, there was some hope amidst the devastation that war caused.

After the procedure was performed, Michelle would return to New York for a short healing period and then undergo another operation before they would have an idea, if any, of success.

Chemah was surprised at how efficiently everything was running in the hospital. He always thought of Israel as a backward country as it was portrayed so many times in the news. He and Michelle were treated with the utmost respect once they were able to find someone in the hospital who was able to speak English. They were taken to the largest wing of the hospital, which was built as a research facility, where they found Dr. Yasmin.

"I received all of your medical information over a month ago," Dr. Yasmin said in perfectly plain English. He spoke to Michelle and looked at Chemah to show him that he was also being regarded in the process. "If all of the information that Dr. Johanson has briefed me about your medical history is accurate, I'll need to do one last examination of my own. After a fresh MRI of your head and a PET scan, we will be able to go forward with the operation."

"I've taken a lot of MRIs in the last few years, but what is a PET scan?"

"Positron emission tomography, or PET for short, is a nuclear medicine imaging technique that produces a three-dimensional image or map of functional processes in the body. The PET scan will take an image of your entire body and show us any abnormalities that we may have to deal with once we're inside."

"Is there anything in particular that you're looking for?" Chemah asked.

"Well, sometimes in these cases, we find that an illness may cause stress or malformation in another area that could hinder the healing process," Dr. Yasmin replied.

Chemah, who had dabbled in Chinese medicine and acupuncture in his earlier studies of the martial arts, was familiar with this idea and nodded his head in understanding. Michelle wasn't as convinced and it showed on her face when she said, "Dr. Johanson told me that everything was already in place. He didn't say anything about more tests."

Chemah reached over to where Michelle's hands lay in her lap and took her hand in his for support. With his eyes, Chemah implored the doctor to say something that would ease Michelle's fear. Dr. Yasmin understood her anxiety and tried to allay her fears by softening his voice.

"I'm sure everything is fine. We simply want to be as prepared as we can be before we go forward."

Michelle took a deep breath and exhaled slowly.

"Okay, where do we start?"

Both Chemah and Dr. Yasmin also exhaled breaths they had been holding for moments without realizing it.

"My nurse has some paperwork for you to sign and then we'll get right to it," Dr. Yasmin said, getting up from his seat.

Chemah helped Michelle up from her seat, smiled at the doctor, and started to lead Michelle toward the door. Michelle abruptly stopped moving, causing Chemah to inadvertently jerk her arm. Michelle gave an annoyed look in Chemah's general direction, then turned to where the doctor still stood.

"What do you suppose the chances are that I'll see again, Doc?"

"I would think that your chances are very good, Ms. Thomas."

Michelle smirked in the doctor's direction.

"Hmm, I wouldn't give a small brown bag full of runny assholes for all the times that I've heard a doctor say that."

The doctor had a good sense of humor. He almost let out a hearty guffaw, but instead coughed and cleared his throat in his attempt to stifle his laughter. Chemah was embarrassed and pulled Michelle's arm toward him. Michelle allowed him to lead her out of the room. She was sure she had gotten at least a smile out of the doctor. All she ever wanted to do was make people laugh and there was no use trying to stop her flow, even way out here in Israel.

Chemah had opted not to eat the airline food served during the last four hours of the flight and was now starving. It would be at least another hour before Michelle would be finished with her tests. Hospital protocol would not allow Chemah to go into the testing area. If he had tried to insist, he knew Michelle would chide him for being overprotective again.

The nurse directed Chemah to the hospital cafeteria and he wound his way slowly through the halls and archways attempting to kill some time before he would have to return to the radiology wing to get Michelle. Chemah ate a knish, which was the only food other than a hamburger that he could identify on the menu. Ironically, in Israel they didn't serve mustard with knishes, and he ate it dry with a diet Coke. Chemah was swallowing his third mouthful when he saw a tall bearded man wearing a checkered overcoat looking at him from the doorway. The moment Chemah noticed him, the man broke into a smile that showed a worn set of teeth. Chemah immediately deduced that the man had spent a lot of time in a desert area. The only thing that could wear a set of teeth down like that was if one ate inordinate amounts of sand with food over long periods of time. As the man did not look like a Syrian nomad, that could only make him military.

Chemah felt his muscles bunch up under his shirt as the man walked toward him. The bearded man stood in front of Chemah. He could easily see the gun that bulged beneath the overcoat. Chemah attempted to stand but the man's voice stopped him.

"*No, pliz seetit down. I am sorry to deesturbit your meal,*" the bearded man apologized in an accent that was not easily identifiable. Chemah detected a bit of German and even some French, but it was definitely not pure Israeli. Since reaching Israel, he'd heard others speak Hebrew and then change to English when they realized he didn't speak Hebrew. None of them had an accent like this guy's.

"*You are Detectif Rivers of New York City, yes?*"

Chemah nodded yes, but was waiting for the man to identify himself before giving out any further information.

"*Forgive my intrusion. I am sure you do not remember me. May I seetit down?*"

The man gestured toward the seat in front of Chemah. Chemah nodded his consent, but watched the man carefully as he sat heavily in the chair.

"*My name is Inspector Yankow, I am with Israeli police,*" he said, flipping open a wallet to show his identification. "*I recognized you earlier when you walked past our morgue.*"

The look on Chemah's face was easily identified as suspicious and the inspector answered his question before he could answer it.

"*Two years ago in New York you come to police academy and give lecture to international police detectives. I was one of three Interpol officers sponsored by the United Nations. We were many men, with many questions, but you answer them all. You were very, how do you say, impressif? Yes, very impressif.*"

"Aah!" Chemah said, slapping his forehead in disgust for not being able to recollect the man. He did, however, remember the event. The United Nations sponsored police officials throughout the Middle East to come to New York City and train with the NYPD for two weeks. At that time, he had just single-handedly apprehended the Jingle Bell murderer. The newspapers were touting him as a modern-day Sherlock Holmes, the man who could find clues where there were no clues to be found.

The academy had used Chemah as a lecturer in the past, and given that Chemah's picture was plastered in the newspapers yet again, the public relations director of the United Nations requested that their guests meet New York's heralded "top cop." Chemah turned out to be a great goodwill ambassador for the city's police force and since then had been redeployed to the academy whenever there were guests from other law enforcement agencies to impress. Chemah didn't mind the extra duty, but was good-naturedly razzed by other detectives whenever he'd been called back to the academy. They called him "golden boy" of all things, but only among themselves, as they were just as loyal to him as he was to them. They all knew he was constantly offered permanent status at the academy and always turned it down.

"I didn't know that Interpol was represented at that training op," Chemah said, sounding interested.

Inspector Yankow shrugged. "*It was unofficial whom I was working for at the time. No matter, it was long time ago and we are here now.*"

Chemah assumed Inspector Yankow was not a stupid man, but thought he was much too trusting. The inspector was giving away official information that could get him into a lot of trouble if the wrong person found out. Now to what end? Chemah sought an answer in the lines above the inspector's brow, as he waited for what would have to be an honest pitch. Chemah nodded and held up a hand, acknowledging that no more need be said on the subject, as he was keenly aware of the delicacy of the inspector's information.

"*If you do not mind my asking, what is it that brings you to Israel, Detectif Rivers?*"

"I'm here with my fiancée. She's having an operation only a specialist here in Israel can perform."

The inspector smiled. "*Yes, we are known to perform such operations that will not yet be performed in the United States of America,*" he said proudly.

Chemah remained silent at this statement, not knowing whether the man was slighting the USA or was just being a proud national. There was a moment's silence between them that was not at all awkward, but one that Chemah would not let go of lest the inspector believe that he had all day to talk.

The inspector's smile slowly dissipated to reveal a grave and concerned look. The veil of friendliness lifted, causing Chemah to think that the man in front of him could win a fortune in Vegas with the type of poker face he had just displayed.

"*I haf a situation, a case that I haf bin working that has bin going very bad, very very bad. When I see you walking down the morgue passage I think maybe God has finally answered my prayers and send you to me.*"

"An answer to your prayers?"

"*I know, it sounds very not prof, prof,,,*"

"Professional?"

"*Yes, no, professional. To be honest, I never in my life haf a prayer answered. But you, you are here. I did not ask for you, but you are here, the man that can find clue where there is no clue. So where else can I look to thank?*" He looked toward the ceiling for emphasis, and Chemah understood his meaning.

"I'm not sure I understand what you are asking, Inspector."

"*I ask merely you look at a body, maybe the crime scene, and tell me what you see.*"

Although slightly intrigued, Chemah shook his head no. "I'm sorry, Inspector, as I told you earlier, I came to Israel for personal reasons." He knew Michelle would go ballistic if she knew he was getting involved with another murder case and looking at dead bodies halfway around the world.

Chemah got up to leave and was startled by the speed and strength with which the man reached out and grabbed his arm, holding him in place. The man was just as startled when Chemah's free hand darted out striking him one-half inch below his elbow. His hand instantly opened, releasing Chemah from his grip, and he was now feeling the complete effect of the strike as his fingers started to tingle and the rest of his arm went numb. He looked up at Chemah and rubbed his arm up and down in an attempt to gain some feeling from it.

"*So, you are a man of many talents*," the inspector said, smiling. This time Chemah knew the smile as the veil that it was.

"It'll be okay in ten or fifteen minutes, keep rubbing it," Chemah said, turning his back.

"*Detectif Rivers*" The inspector raised his voice so that others close to his seat turned to look. "*What if I were to say there are five bodies for you to examine*?"

Chemah didn't turn immediately, but then thought of the implication. He turned around slowly and saw that the inspector's poker face was no longer in place. The man looked miserable and totally worn down.

"*Could you turn your back then*?"

Chemah walked back to the table and sat down in front of the inspector.

"All the same killer?"

"*We believe so. Or maybe cult killing*."

Chemah grimaced. "Give me your arm."

The inspector looked suspiciously at Chemah. "*Don't worry, it will be fine,*" the inspector offered.

"No, it won't be fine," Chemah said, reaching across the table for the arm that was dangling lifelessly at the inspector's side.

"I lied, it won't be better in fifteen minutes. There's no permanent damage to it, but the feeling would probably come around in more like fifteen days."

"*You do not like to be touched, the way I touch you, yes*." The inspector smiled as he allowed Chemah to manipulate his arm.

"No, I don't like to be touched the way you touched me, no," Chemah said as he savagely twisted the man's arm into an awkward position and struck it on the same pressure point one-half inch below the elbow.

The scream that came from the inspector was not unmanly, just that of a man in blinding pain. This time, everyone in the cafeteria turned and looked their way. Some of the people got up and walked out, their instincts for trouble quite acute, having been honed as a result of so many years of living in a country constantly at war.

The inspector tore his arm away from Chemah's grasp and in doing so realized that he could indeed feel it again. He rubbed it a few more times for good measure, assuring himself that Chemah had not caused further damage. His sand-ground teeth smiled gruesomely and the twinkle in his eyes returned when he realized there was no numbness and no pain.

"*Yes, a man of many talents*," he said aloud to no one in particular, all the while flexing and relaxing his arm, unsure of its use.

Chemah looked at his watch. There would be little time to see the bodies in question if he were going to be there when Michelle finished her PET. A second look at his watch changed his mind entirely.

"My fiancée's surgery is tomorrow. According to her surgeon the procedure should take approximately seven hours. Could you arrange for all the bodies to be available in the morgue tomorrow at about eight o'clock in the morning?"

"*Yes, all of the bodies will be there waiting. We had a sixth, but the family strictly insisted that Jewish custom be observed and she was buried the day after she was found.*"

"Six bodies and there was no mention of it in the news?"

"*You will know why when you see the bodies.*"

The inspector's smile went away again at the mention of the bodies. This time the transformation in his face made goose bumps form on the back of Chemah's neck and the hair on his arms stand at attention.

Chapter 3

Wash Your Hands Before Leaving

The next day Chemah kissed Michelle good-bye and wished her luck on the bridge of the seventh floor that separated the waiting room from the operating room.

"I'll be right here when you come out, baby," he assured her.

"I'll keep an eye out for you," Michelle said.

It was a joke that they had shared on the first day they met and it never got old for either one of them. Chemah continued to laugh as she was wheeled away by the orderly and blew her a kiss that no one but the hospital ghosts would see.

The minute she was out of sight Chemah headed to the morgue. He knew exactly where it was, having passed it the day before while taking his own little tour of the facilities.

Inspector Yankow was waiting for him with two other men who wore long white lab coats. Chemah knew these men would be the medical examiner and someone from the police department's forensics team. The bodies were already in place, each on a separate table lined up in the center of the room. The bodies were covered from head to toe by thin white sheets. Chemah could already see that some of the sheets were stuck to the bodies at odd places where blood had seeped through. It was a morbid thought, but he was glad to see that the blood was clinging to the sheets. That meant that someone had the foresight not to clean the bodies too thoroughly before someone with his experience could have a look.

According to Jewish law, after death, the body is to be buried as soon as possible. If an autopsy is performed, all of the organs must be returned to the body. Then the body is placed in another body sack, ensuring that every part of the human form is buried with its owner. The custom is so strict that Chemah knew that even the sheets that held the tiniest vestiges of the victim's blood would have to be buried with the body.

The formal introductions were over and Chemah wasted no time. He walked over to the sink and performed his ritual hand and arm scrub. After drying his hands he was handed a pair of latex gloves by the medical examiner. Yankow was already hovering over a body and Chemah knew it was the first one he wanted Chemah to examine. Chemah walked to the body, took a deep breath, and slowly lifted the sheet off of the corpse. It was a thirty-something-year-old man. Chemah surmised that the three-inch-long rips in the man's face were made by long fingernails, possibly those of a woman. As he pulled the sheet farther down he saw the bulge in the neck that meant that the neck had been broken. He pulled the sheet farther down and discerned other broken bones—bones broken so cleanly that they protruded through the skin, but were barely jagged. Chemah instantly thought, *hammer*, then changed his mind when he saw the impossibility of the angles. *Nothing out of the ordinary other than the scratches on the face*. Chemah had seen many dead bodies, but this one gave him a feeling of déjà vu. The body was almost familiar to him. Chemah shrugged his shoulders trying to shake the familiar feeling.

"He was beaten with something blunt. Some of the bruises to his face would indicate that he was slapped around a little." Chemah pulled the sheet the rest of the way off and continued to examine the corpse, touching and tapping protruding parts of each appendage. There were many tests that he would have wanted to perform, but he was only here for a general once-over. Everything that he would have wanted done would take at least two weeks considering the number of bodies.

Chemah moved on to the next body without covering the first one that he examined. The outline of the sheet showed large breasts, and long hair fell out from beneath the sheet. Chemah hid his emotions well. No one could ever tell how disturbed he was when he viewed female corpses. The smell of this one nauseated him more than the previous, only because she was female. He knew it was a psychosomatic trick of his mind and concentrated harder on the woman's wounds in an effort to isolate the trauma from the identity of the person who might once have dwelled in this now defunct shell.

Inspector Yankow allowed Chemah to view and handle each body, searching Chemah's face every moment for a sign that a discovery was made. To the inspector's delight Chemah's face did not show a hint of emotion when the second, third, or even fifth body showed identical wounds.

Chemah finished his visual of the bodies and turned to speak directly to the inspector, unsure if the other two men understood enough English to answer any questions.

"If you checked underneath the fingernails of the woman on the second table you might find some tissue from the face of that man on the first table. Her nails look like they would be a perfect match for those marks on his face. A possibility that he was her attacker and was scratched in the midst of a struggle."

"We haf already checked her fingernails and haf matched his DNA with the material that we found beneath them. That is why we haf zuch a dilemma. You see, he was found dead before she. We haf done more investigation than maybe you think we are capable of? The bruises on his body, the face, the crushed skull, they haf been matched against a cast imprint of her fist. They are a perfect match." The inspector gestured with an open hand

at the female corpse. *"She killed him,"* he said in a matter-of-fact fashion.

For the first time since he started examining the bodies, Chemah could not hide his surprise. He looked back and forth at the first two bodies he had examined and then went back to the first corpse again. This time he adjusted the magnifying glass that was attached to the table so that it hovered above the neck of the victim. After a minute of looking through the glass he adjusted it again over the wrist of the victim and then moments later above the victim's ankle. Chemah shook his head emphatically at the corpse that now posed an enigma.

Inspector Yankow sidled up to Chemah, who was now biting his bottom lip in open frustration. "*We also do not see what you are looking for.*"

Chemah turned to the inspector to confirm that they were both on the same page.

"He has no markings to show that he was restrained during the assault that caused his death," the inspector confirmed.

Chemah bit his lip harder when the confirmation was made and winced openly as the metallic taste of his own blood touched the most sensitive surface of his tastebuds. It didn't make any sense. This man was over a hundred pounds heavier than the woman and he seemed to have been in pretty good shape. A thought crossed Chemah's mind as the only thing that made any sense.

"Did you check his blood for any drugs that he might have taken or that may have been administered to him?"

"His blood was checked. It showed nothing unusual."

"And the woman?"

The inspector smiled. *"Only one thing."*

Chemah waited.

"The adrenaline in her blood was far beyond levels of normalcy or anything the lab had ever seen. They checked for outside stimulus, but found nothing. Her hypothalamus, pituitary, and adrenal glands were burnt out,

as though they combusted while producing adrenaline. But nothing more."

"Nothing more? That sounds like everything right there."

The inspector shook his head sadly, as if disappointed in Chemah.

"That answers but a fraction of the questions that we haf here, and even that makes no sense. For instance, you suspect as I did that the woman may haf gained the strength to assault and then kill this man through the elevated adrenaline levels, whether it was caused naturally or gained by other means." The inspector took a deep breath and then exhaled through his nose, snorting like a disgruntled bull. *"As you might haf guessed already, there are many details that I purposely did not afford you. You must forgive me. I did not want your observation to be tainted by elements that I myself found to be inconsequential. But now I must tell you the things that will make your summation useless to us."* The inspector snorted again. *"The man on the table iz a highly decorated officer in our military. He was an instructor of Krav Magar."* Chemah's eyebrow raised at this information. Being a Karate Master himself, he was aware of other deadly martial arts utilized around the world. Krav Magar was a vicious martial art developed by the Israeli army that did away with other flowery movements that the older martial arts used. From the few demonstrations that Chemah had seen, he knew that anyone who was an instructor for the military must have been a deadly man.

"The woman that you see here was a clothing model. No military training. She came from a well-to-do family. He should haf been able to incapacitate her in his sleep, even if she was injected with high-grade PCP."

Chemah turned to look at the model again, using only a nod to acknowledge that he concurred with the inspector.

"What about the other three? Were any of their adrenaline levels elevated?"

"Sadly, no. That would haf been a major break for our case, would you not say?"

Chemah nodded again, but still kept his eye on the model's body. Something about her was still very familiar to him as well, although he could not quite put his finger on it. After a moment he felt his head throbbing from trying to figure it out. It was no use. He knew the way his mind worked. It would come to him later. Chemah looked at his watch. Only ninety minutes had passed. It would be another four hours before Michelle would be finished in the operating room.

"I believe I've told you all that I can about your victims given the time constraints, inspector. I have another three hours before I have to leave you," he said, looking at his watch again for confirmation. "Maybe if you showed me one or two of the crime scenes I could be of more help."

"Yes, of course. We are not far away. Two of the crime scenes are within thirty minutes of this hospital."

The inspector signaled to the other two men who waited off to the side. They stepped forward simultaneously to cover the victim's bodies again. The men began talking among themselves before the Inspector and Chemah left the room. The inspector turned back to give them a stern look that silenced both of the men instantly. Chemah took notice of the gesture and took a last look back at the two men covering the bodies.

It was from this vantage point that Chemah finally saw the pattern that eluded him when he was directly in front of the bodies. It was the grouping of the bodies that was ultimately familiar.

Chemah looked at the inspector quizzically and one whispered word escaped his lips. "Fallujah?"

The inspector's faith was restored with this one word. The look on the man's face let Chemah know the inspector understood exactly what he was thinking. He could only draw the conclusion that the inspector had been holding back even more information than he finally divulged earlier.

"What was that, Detectif Rivers?" the inspector said, trying to disguise his knowledge and joy at what Chemah had finally figured out.

"You know. You knew all along and didn't tell me." Chemah didn't hide his irritation at being played.

"Of what do you speak? I do not know." The inspector shrugged his shoulders.

Chemah was not angry. It was obvious to him why he was not told. Now he realized why this inspector who originated from Interpol was in charge of the investigation.

Chemah started to walk back toward the bodies. The inspector, who was following closely behind, motioned for the two men who had assisted to leave the room.

"It was in all the major newspapers for months last year. It even made the cover of *Time* magazine. These people were murdered in the same way that the American soldier in Fallujah who was accused of raping a girl and killing her five family members committed his crimes. They said he killed the family members just to cover up the rape."

"Iz that so?"

Chemah didn't bother to answer using the sarcasm that he felt. He knew that the inspector wouldn't confirm or deny the allegation.

"How do you know thiz information? I understand that it iz highly classified."

"Classified? The pictures of the massacre are all over the Internet."

The inspector wasn't moved by this information. Chemah suspected that this might be the man who had already dealt with whoever it was that leaked the pictures.

"You told me earlier that I would know why the public was not aware of these murders."

"*Iz that what I said?"* The inspector feigned innocence.

Chemah ignored his act. "If the Israeli government acknowledges these murders as duplicates of the murders in Fallujah, they would either have to blame the U.S. military for the atrocities or blame the Iraqis for retaliation. Blame the U.S. and you lose their support. Blame the Iraqis and the peace talks are gone for a very long time. Your people would expect your president to do his own retaliation for these acts and that would not be to his best interest at this time, am I right?"

The inspector would not answer even this simple question. He merely smiled and shrugged his shoulders.

"Yeah, that's what I thought," Chemah said, understanding the meaning of this stupid gesture. "Do you still want me to see to those crime scenes?" he said, looking up from the bodies again.

"Of course, Detectif Rivers. Your expertise iz still a value to us at thiz time."

Chemah shrugged this time. He was intrigued by this case, but his mind was starting to veer toward Michelle's welfare as the time for the completion of her operation drew nearer.

Chemah headed for the door again, with the inspector moving along just behind him. Two feet from the door Chemah stopped again and turned to the inspector.

"I couldn't really tell from the pictures on the Internet, but it's clear to me now that there is a pattern to the bone breaks."

"Yes, the same bones were broken, again and again in each case."

"You misunderstand me, Inspector. Not the duplication of bones that were broken. The pattern that the breaking of those bones creates."

The look on the inspector's face made Chemah realize that he had discovered something that the inspector and his team had not.

"The way that the broken bones are ordered makes the peace sign symbol." Chemah pulled his pen and a piece of paper from his pocket and drew the symbol for the inspector.

The Inspector's brow was creased in worry. He should have seen the symbol and he had not. "In a place where there iz no peace, I would say that whoever iz responsible for these acts is hafing a little joke at the expense of their victims."

Chemah put the piece of paper away and took the two steps to the door. As he turned the knob he heard the door on the other side of the room open and didn't bother to turn and see the inspector's two men come into the room again. He knew the inspector would be signaling to them to clean up.

He looked at his watch again. He'd have to hurry now. There was no way he was going to be late. He promised Michelle he would be there when she woke from the anesthetic.

Chapter 4

In Full View

"There now, Mrs. Thomas, are you comfortable?" the nurse asked while pulling a light blanket across Michelle's legs.

"Yup! Snug as a bug in a rug. Only it's not *Mrs.* Thomas, it's *Miss,*" Michelle replied.

Michelle could not see the surprise in the woman's face, but could hear it in her voice.

"The man with the beautiful eyes, he is not your husband?"

Michelle had never heard anyone remark on Chemah's eyes, but knew she must be talking about him.

"Nope, not my husband—that would make me Mrs. Rivers." Michelle would never admit it, but she liked when people made the mistake of calling her "Mrs. Rivers." Back home, in the States, it happened often and she never took the opportunity to correct anyone. *Mrs. Michelle Rivers. That sounds so right and has a really nice ring to it!*

"Very well, then, I am Tirzah. I will be here to take care of only you."

The nurse smiled, although she had no idea how bugs in rugs brought comfort. *Americans, they are quite interesting.*

"You will feel only sleepy in a moment. I am giving you something to help you rest," she said, checking the small plastic pouch that dripped its contents steadily into the tube imbedded in Michelle's arm. "Please continue to rest quietly. I will be sitting right outside the testing chamber to your left should you need me."

"Thank you," Michelle replied, not wanting to say another word as she had to concentrate on fighting back tears.

She had given Chemah her best "it's all good" impersonation so that he wouldn't worry, or worse, force the techs into letting him stay in the examination area. Chemah's love had brought Michelle a long way and she trusted him more than anyone in the world. She wasn't ready to admit that herself, or to him. She felt exposed and vulnerable, scared shitless at the prospect of being able to see again.

While Michelle desperately wanted to see Chemah, she prayed that sight wouldn't dull the other senses that became acute during their love-making. The sound of his voice as he whispered in her ear while entering her, the taste of the sweat that dripped from him, the urgency of his touch, his scent—these were the things Michelle was not ready to forfeit for the sake of sight.

C'mon, girl, get a grip. This is not the time or place for you to start crying like a baby. She was fighting the sedative she was receiving intravenously, trying desperately to stay awake until he arrived to tell her things were still all right. To relax herself, she allowed her thoughts to settle on Chemah. She thought about how he had literally saved her life from that maniacal serial killer, the Street Sweeper. She hadn't known at the time that with his patience and compassion he was saving her so that he could cleave her to his own soul. Michelle had been grounded in her resolve to be emotionally impregnable and she was heavily armed with a quick wit and a wickedly sharp tongue. Chemah had pulled her away from that space. He was her air, her source of strength and confidence. Her love for Héro and Tatsuya was an extension of her love for Chemah. She adored those children and their father, absolutely and completely.

Michelle knew she loved Chemah from day one. She would have called it love at first sight if she could see a damned thing. Irony, if ever there was such a thing. Her stable life and carefully controlled emotions had become a crazy roller-coaster ride into the unknown from the moment she contacted him and it hadn't changed since that day.

Michelle's languid smile was a telltale sign of the thoughts she harbored for Chemah as she lay on the examination table. Her breathing became shallow and she allowed the slight warmth that she felt between her legs whenever she thought about Chemah to comfort her as she drifted off into a drug-induced slumber.

Moments after she dozed, Chemah entered the hospital room. He'd arrived at the hospital much later than he intended and he ran up the six flights of stairs to save time. The nurse outside Michelle's room noticed the slick sheen of sweat that beaded his forehead and the thick pulsating vein that ran from his upper jaw to his clavicle. She nodded to him in recognition as he stepped quickly inside the room. He was glad to see that Michelle was still under sedation and could feel his steel-hard muscles relax at the realization that he had gotten there before she awakened from the operation.

Chemah walked to the side of the bed and kissed Michelle gently on the lips. Her dreamy smile spread only slightly, but Chemah took no notice. Now that he knew Michelle was well, his mind was already refocusing on the bodies that he had viewed earlier.

The inspector was reluctant to allow Chemah to send photos of the bodies to one of his co-workers in the States, but Chemah convinced him that if he wanted a swift answer to the configuration of the bone breaks, they should send them to the one person he knew was an expert in bone fragmentation. The inspector argued that their own experts had already viewed the broken bones. All it took was a look from Chemah to remind the inspector that he was able to discern a pattern that had not been distinguishable to the Israeli experts.

Chemah stepped back out into the corridor and looked for the waiting room but all the signs were written in Hebrew. Chemah turned to the nurse who was sitting outside Michelle's door. She was already looking up at him, anxious to be of some help. Chemah pulled out his cell phone and started to dial.

"Is there somewhere private I could use?"

The nurse got up from her seat and motioned for him to follow her. Chemah already had the phone to his ear and was listening to ringing when the nurse stopped in front of a room and motioned him into the doorway. It was a waiting room like any other in the States. Chemah mouthed the words, "thank you," as the ringing continued on the other end. The nurse only nodded and gave Chemah a knowing glance. She chanced a rearview look at Chemah and sighed in appreciation of his broad back that narrowed perfectly at his waist and tight ass. As beautiful as he was, she knew that she could never be with such a man in Israel. "*Schvartze*," they would call him. It meant "black beast." Modern Israel was tolerant of many new ideas, but the issue of color was one that, like in the United States, was hidden behind the differences in religious beliefs. "He will never understand your people," they had told the friend who fell in love with an African American soldier. When she did not give in, she was shunned and ostracized from her family. At the thought, Tirzah walked quickly away from the room that Chemah entered and looked around nervously, concerned that someone may have seen her look at Chemah in such a way.

The phone rang for the tenth time and a sleepy voice answered.

"Mmmm, yo, we sleepin'. Who the fuck this is?"

Chemah smiled at the sound of the voice and the vernacular he knew so well. Rob was the only white man he knew who spoke in the colloquial dialect of someone who had grown up in the blackest part of Harlem. In fact, Chemah had lived in Harlem all his life and had not heard anyone sound quite as "hood" as Rob. Chemah didn't mind it much. He knew Rob was harmless and wasn't trying to clown blacks. He actually once asked Rob about the hood talk and Rob clearly did not understand that there was any difference other than maybe a slight accent in the way that they each spoke. Chemah had finally figured it out at a barbecue that Rob had given last year.

Apparently Rob's parents had taken in a foster child when Rob was only ten years old. The boy, also named Robert, was two years older than Rob. He was African American and was previously raised in the not-so-genteel South Bronx. Chemah met Robert at the barbecue. He was a Harvard-educated doctor, and Rob still looked up to him. He didn't talk the way that Rob did unless Rob was near enough to hear him. Chemah thought it was a shame that someone whom Rob introduced as his brother was such a phony. However, that was family business and Chemah was not trying to involve himself in that. The real shame of it was that Rob's two pre-pubescent boys also spoke that way and because of their total immersion in the hip-hop culture, they thought that this was an appropriate way of speaking.

At the precinct Rob's co-workers called him "Black Rob." Rob thought it was cool. He didn't know they were making fun of him and Chemah never had the heart to tell him the truth.

"It's me, Rob, Chemah."

"Hey, Chem? What's happenin', son? Damn, what time is it?"

"Six in the evening, here in Israel. That would make it about two in the morning there. Sorry to call so late, but it couldn't be helped."

"I just creeped in about an hour ago. My lady is pissed. Every time you ask me to do something it jams me up with my people."

"You could always say no, Rob. It's not like I wouldn't understand."

"Yo, yo, come on, son! You know I'm not going to say no to you. You and me, we go way back, like reclining chairs."

"Thanks, Rob, I appreciate that."

Rob blushed on the other end. He was proud that Chemah considered him a friend and that he could be of help. Chemah was always friendly and considerate to other cops and co-workers on the job, but he kept most people at arm's length. Rob was one of the few people whom Chemah considered a friend and everyone on the job knew it. Rob knew everyone made fun of the way he spoke—everyone except Chemah.

"What about those jpegs I sent you? Were you able to make any sense of them?"

"I was able to micro-synthesize the photos so that I could look at them clearly under the nuclear microscope for any abnormalities. Guess what I found?"

"What?" Chemah's breath caught in his chest in a moment of excitement over a possible lead.

"Nathin'."

Chemah's breath left his lungs slowly, leaving him feeling deflated.

"Nothing? No conspicuous fragments? No cellular decomposition, nothing peculiar?"

"Not a muthafuckin' thing. The only thing that could be confirmed was exactly what you said—the bones were broken by someone's hands. The stress fractures on either side of every bone show that the breaks weren't arbitrary an' shit. Na'sayin'?"

"Yeah, who ever did this shit was one strong sumbitch."

Chemah didn't want to tell Rob that each body might have had a different killer. That would extend the conversation to one that was longer than Chemah wanted to have. Although Rob did sound ignorant sometimes, he was an excellent forensic scientist and he took his job very seriously. It was one of the reasons he and Chemah got along so well. They could both spend hours sifting through evidence that others would find tedious.

When Chemah didn't say anything else, Rob continued.

"What I did find interesting was the pictures of the bodies that you sent me. I wanted to ask you, was there any particular reason why you thought that the bones were being broken to form a peace sign?"

The pattern had been obvious to Chemah and now he wondered why it wasn't obvious to Rob. The conversation was wearing thin, so he asked plainly, "What do you think it is, Rob?"

"To me it looks like an upside-down cross."

"You think it's a satanic symbol?"

"Son, you been watching too many horror flicks. An upside-down cross isn't just symbolic of Satan. If I ain't got nothin' else from my twelve years of Catholic school and being an altar boy, it's that ain't shit ever what you think it is, when it comes to God."

Rob paused for effect, but Chemah waited him out knowing that Rob was only too happy to show that he had information that Chemah didn't.

"In the first century around sixty-four A.D, which happened to be around the time of the great fire of Rome, when Nero was the emperor, St. Peter was sentenced to be crucified for trying to spread the gospel of Christ. Peter's only request was that he be crucified upside-down, because he thought that he was not worthy to be crucified the way that his Master, Jesus, had been. Since St. Peter there's been a shitload of dudes who also happened to be martyrs or saints and have made the same request. A lot of people don't know it, but the Pope actually sits in a chair that is marked with the upside-down cross in memory of St. Peter, who was the only apostle who ever made it to Rome. Every Pope who has ever been in Rome since is said to be the spiritual successor of Peter."

This was absolutely news to Chemah, whose only experience with religion ended when his grandmother took him to an Apostolic church when he was six and he begged his mother never to send him back, because he was frightened of all the old ladies who jumped into the aisles crying and talking in a strange language that sounded almost like the crazy Spanish lady down the street who cursed everybody who passed her stoop.

"So this Saint Peter, he was Jesus' best Apostle?

"Are you kidding me? Peter was always fucking up. Have you ever heard the saying, 'Get behind me, Satan'?"

"Yeah, my grandmother used to say that to my grandfather all the time."

"Well, the story goes that Jesus said to Peter, 'Get behind me, Satan, you are a stumbling block. You are not on the side of God, but of men.' Or something like that. He was also the one that Jesus had to tell 'If you live by the sword, you will die by the sword.' He said this after Peter cut off a Roman soldier's ear. Anyway, you get my point. Pete was a fuck-up."

"So this upside-down cross of St. Peter, what do you think it has to do with the bodies?"

"Shit, dog, you just went right outside my expertise with that one. Far as I can see, not a damn thing. All 'cept the obvious, that the bodies being broken up to resemble this cross just happen to be in arguably the most holy country in the world."

Chemah and the inspector had already put that spin on it, but that was when they had thought that the bones were being broken into peace signs.

"Yeah, I got that."

"Yo, how long you stayin' out there, son? You not tryin' to stay out there until they figure this shit out, are you?" Before Chemah could answer, Rob was rambling. "Son, son, you better watch your back out there. Ain't like you got a nigga like me ridin' with you like we do in the N.Y.C. Na'mean?"

"Rob, I told you about using the word nig–"

"I hear you, I hear what you sayin', son, but it don't count if I'm talking 'bout me, right?"

"I don't have time for this right now, Rob. For the last time, I'm warning you, keep that word out of your mouth."

"A'ight, a'ight, but I'm bringin' back *knucka*. Ain't nobody ever had a problem with *knucka*, right?"

Chemah hung up on him. He sensed someone behind him and turned to see the nurse assigned to Michelle waving to him through the glass window in the waiting room door.

"Is she awake?"

The nurse couldn't hear him through the door, but read his lips and nodded to confirm that Michelle had awakened again.

Chemah opened the waiting room door and rushed to his right. He pushed Michelle's hospital room door open and was startled to see Michelle attempting to rip the white gauze bandages away from her eyes. Chemah rushed to her bedside and grabbed both her hands in his. "Chemah, Chemah, is that you?" Michelle said, slurring her words. It was obvious the medication she was on was having some sort of adverse effect.

"It's me, baby," Chemah said, loosening his grip, but not letting her go.

"I can see, sweetheart, I can see!"

Chemah looked to the nurse, who was now on the other side of the bed, with a questioning glance. In return he got a sad shake of her head.

"Try to relax, Michelle. Leave the bandages on a little longer." Chemah attempted to placate her as he watched the nurse add what he could only guess was more of whatever sedative or pain reliever they were using on her, to the intravenous device that was already attached to her arm. Almost as soon as the nurse was finished, Chemah could feel Michelle go limp in his hands. She lay back against the pillows behind her and a dreamy smile played on her lips.

"She will sleep longer now," the nurse said, picking up the chart and making a notation before placing it back at the foot of the bed.

Chemah felt his own tension ease and he allowed himself to sit carefully on the side of Michelle's bed. He tried to mimic the smile that he saw on Michelle's face, but couldn't. The image of the bodies that he'd seen at the morgue haunted him.

Chapter 5

On the Way Home

The flight attendant caught herself staring at the striking couple seated in the front row of first class. She was in the back of the plane preparing food when they first boarded and now, seeing them up close, was unsure if they were even a couple. The beautiful green-eyed black man with the dreadlocks was engrossed in a file and the stunningly beautiful woman next to him with the perfect caramel skin wearing sunglasses appeared to be looking out the window while listening to an iPod. Michelle was actually listening to a book titled *The Last Prejudice*. She was totally engrossed in what she was listening to and did not hear when the attendant asked, "Madam, may I offer you a beverage?"

Chemah nudged Michelle and reached over and pulled one of the plugs out of her ear without bothering to look up away from the file in his lap. Michelle was startled out of her silence and turned her face away from the sun that radiated through the small portal that the airlines called a window. She enjoyed the sun on her face through a closed window. She often sat at a closed window at home, absorbing the magnified rays of the sun as they left her skin with the sensation of having been caressed with a warm feather.

The attendant was embarrassed and dismayed when Michelle looked up toward her but spoke to a space several inches away from where her face actually was. Michelle was used to the awkward moment of silence when someone realized she was blind and waited the brief moment it took the attendant to compose herself and repeat her question.

"Would you like a beverage, ma'am?"

Michelle wasn't thirsty, but ordered a ginger ale anyway.

Bereft watched the scene unfold from his seat just a row away to the left of Michelle and Chemah. He watched Chemah's casual and calm manner and openly sneered in his direction.

At the moment, he inhabited the body of a young Jewish businessman. He'd followed Chemah and Michelle from the hospital, jumping from body to body to get this close. This last body he secured when they called for first-class boarders over the loud speaker. Chemah and the Jewish businessman got up at the same time and when the man saw that Michelle was blind, he allowed Chemah to go first. Bereft entered the man as he stood just behind Chemah in the line. He immediately felt queasy and knew the cause was the gold Star of David that hung loosely around the man's neck. Bereft reached into the top of the tunic that he wore and grasped the medal in his palm. He knew that the medal could do him no real harm without the faith of the man to draw from it, but his repulsion of the symbol was still strong. He allowed it to slide carelessly out of his hand while waiting to board the airplane. No one noticed as it slid noiseless around on the floor, being kicked from one foot to the next.

Bereft knew what a plane was, having garnered the information from the memories of the first body he possessed when he unexpectedly found his freedom just over a year ago. Until now, he did not feel the need to travel in this new fashion that men had conjured. He had never enjoyed long voyages, once having spent two months on a barge traveling from Kemet to Jerusalem. Having only the minds and bodies of the thirty-seven people on that voyage to toy with left him with an aversion to isolating himself like that again. Since then he stayed on land where bodies and minds were plentiful until Sodom.

Bereft thought of entering Chemah for the thousandth time since having felt his presence in the hospital. He was drawn to the light that shone through Chemah, recognizing it as the same ethereal power that had pulsed through and around the man called Lot so many thousands of years ago. Although it was not half or a fifth or even a hundredth of the power that had emanated from Lot, nonetheless it was a power and light that was easily identifiable. Bereft smiled to himself as he looked over at Chemah and wondered if Chemah could be one of Lot's descendants. Having taken the body of a Hebrew scholar some months ago, Bereft learned that Lot had besmirched his name by having children with his own daughters. Since then, the lineage of those who came after Lot was lost. It was only by chance that he saw and felt the light that came from Chemah when he was about to take the body of the man who was following the trail of his most recent fun. He left the bodies entangled with the symbol that the scholar he had originally taken found to be of the utmost importance. The first time he did it was only for the fun and irony of it. With the attention that it drew, he found it amusing and did it over and over again. The symbol itself meant nothing to him. The god that it was meant to symbolize was unknown to him. It was the God of Abraham whose power Bereft was after. Seeing Chemah, he knew it still existed. After these thousands of years it made him blind with rage.

Chemah was reviewing a copy of the file that Inspector Yankow gave him after they examined the most recent victim's body. It was given to him with the understanding that no one else would see it and that he would study it until he found some other lead that had yet to be seen.

A disconcerting feeling came over Chemah as he tried to concentrate and he turned, looking over his shoulder, and found the eyes of a young dark-haired man. The man smiled, but Chemah saw no good intent in him. The man turned away from Chemah's stare and Chemah closed the folder, deciding that maybe it was the thing that had him on edge. Michelle was still listening to her book and Chemah picked up one of her hands to hold, expecting the warmth and calm that she brought with her when she was of a calm mind. Michelle turned to him and smiled, leaning toward him with pouting lips that Chemah kissed softly feeling her warmth spreading through him. The bad feeling he had experienced melted away as Michelle drew closer to him, taking his other hand in hers.

Bereft was repulsed at the sight of Chemah's and Michelle's public display of affection and was of a mind to enter Michelle's body. But, he foresaw that Chemah would know him too soon if he did this and ground the teeth of the body he possessed to keep himself focused. For all the years that he inhabited the earth and all the power that he wielded, Bereft was still susceptible to the petty emotions of a thinking entity. He was still filled with jealousy. He had very little self-control and was still very audacious. What other word could be used to describe wanting the power that only God could wield and give, if not *audacious*?

Bereft looked at the couple sitting behind Michelle and Chemah and smiled sadistically. Here were two people whom he would take great joy in destroying. They were newlyweds returning from their honeymoon, and still feeling the passion of two who had not coupled during their engagement. Bereft watched and listened to them for the entire flight. He was only slightly disappointed that the woman was no longer a virgin. He could smell the blood of her recently deflowered vagina and although the smell was days old, it still raised small bumps on the possessed body's flesh. Bereft teased himself for hours thinking of what he would do with the man and woman. He would take one and then the other, making each do things that the other would never have imagined and at the end, leave them both unable to bear the unspeakable things they'd done, ending their marriage in misery. The thought alone made Bereft's breath hard with anxiety and he ground his teeth again, waiting for the moment when he could show his true nature. As he waited and planned, Bereft thought of the anger that he would face from his brother Loki, if Loki only knew that he was impinging on victims from Loki's own territory. The language of these people was surely descended from the Norse. Loki had chosen and marked his territory clearly early on when he chose to play in the lives of the golden-haired people. The skin of these two was as white as any he had seen in the eons that he lived. The man was taller than any man on this so-called "plane" and the woman taller than any woman. When first he was released from his prison he tried to sense his other brothers to no avail. He should have been able to sense at least one of his brothers from a thousand leagues away, for they all played the same games in one way or another, but alas, he could not. If Loki knew that he was tampering with souls from his territory there would be much to atone for, but looking at the two golden-haired specimens, Bereft felt no fear of his missing brother's wrath. He was ready to play.

The couple, Bereft learned their names were Leif and Hayley, played beneath the small woolen blanket that connected them in the spacious seats in first class. Their plan was childish if not stupid, thought Bereft, as he listened keenly to the whispering and giggling they had done for the tiresome hours of the flight. As they reached closer to their destination they would leave their seats, one behind the other, to meet in the small shit room and make love.

How pathetic, he thought, trying to drive his own panic from his mind.

Bereft knew from his victim's memory that the flight was nineteen hours long, and he was unnerved by the amount of time to be spent over the water. If the plane went down there would be no help for him. The salt in the water would drive him out of this body and it would most assuredly bury him for a long while in its depths.

Oh, but the prize will be great if my plan is seen through, he pondered as he saw Hayley finally leave her seat, winking at Leif as she turned and made her way up the aisle toward the shit room.

Leif waited a few moments and got up from his seat, trying his best to be inconspicuous. As he passed the man seated alone across from him and his wife, the man opened his eyes and nonchalantly reached out to touch him. Instantly, Bereft transferred himself into Leif. This body was much more comfortable to Bereft. The previous body had been soaked with fermented fluids and there was very little reserve energy to use to make this body stronger or enhance his senses. This Norseman's body was stronger and more to his liking. It would only last a week or so if he stayed in it, but at this moment it was more than he needed. He looked to the body that he just left. The man was unconscious, his breathing was shallow, and sweat came out of his pores profusely. He would live, but his health would never be the same. Bereft had no other thought of him.

Bereft walked down the aisle without a care for who saw him, but no one did. Everyone he passed was asleep. What chaos he could cause in this enclosed space, he thought briefly, then thought better, remembering the saltwater beneath him. He stopped in front of the shit room door and sniffed the air hard once to find the scent of a freshly broken cunt. It was his favorite smell and he knew it was behind the door to the left. An old lady with bladder incontinence and diarrhea was behind the door to the right.

Bereft rapped on the door twice with the knuckles of his right hand and the door was immediately opened by Hayley. She smiled up at him as she let him through the door, closing it quickly behind them. Bereft saw in her face that she instantly felt there was something wrong. There was something different about Leif's eyes. Nevertheless, Hayley flung her arms around her husband's neck and reached up to kiss him. Bereft did not move. He neither helped her nor hindered her, standing erect and stiff as she attempted to cajole him with her body. Hayley wrapped one of her long slender legs around his and ground her pelvis against his hips.

"I already took my panties off," she admitted, pulling her skirt up to expose her full-lipped vagina covered by a patch of sparse blonde hair. Bereft looked down at the covered vulva and smiled. Now that he was closer to it, the smell was almost overwhelming. Hayley reached up and pulled against her husband's neck, attempting to force his mouth down to hers. When she realized that he wouldn't be moved, she climbed his body, wrapping her legs around his waist. When her tongue slipped between his lips Bereft bit it hard, causing her to whimper and pull back. When she looked again, she saw what she thought was the sadistic gleam that got into her husband's eyes when they played naughty games. If she only knew better, she'd have seen it was pure Bereft.

"I know what you want. You want *der after* again, don't you?" Hayley said, climbing down from her husband's body. She turned her back to Bereft and lifted her skirt to show the two perfectly formed globes of her white ass.

Bereft took a moment to look into Leif's memory and saw what he was looking for. It was the reason why this woman was so amicable to being sodomized and why she was only recently deflowered.

Hayley and Leif were meant for each other. Leif had a hint of mischievousness in him and preferred to anally sodomize his lovers, causing some pain to satisfy his sadistic nature. Hayley confessed to her husband early on that she loved to be hurt, having been paddled by the father she adored as a teenager whenever she did something wrong to get his attention. Hayley's ass had always been the focus of their attention during lovemaking. They only recently used her vagina for sex on their honeymoon to consummate their vows but it had held only limited pleasure for both of them.

Bereft looked between Hayley's ass cheeks and spit deliberately on the aperture that formed the ring of her asshole. It was his nature to bring pleasure before bringing pain but now he was mad at both having been cooped up in this plane and having the threat of saltwater lingering beneath him for so long. Without waiting for the moisture that he applied to settle into her ass, Bereft plunged his index finger and forefinger deep into her rectum, stopping only when the width of the rest of his hand would allow for no further entry. Hayley's face was pressed into the wall of the small room and she mewled noisily for only a moment before she realized that any loud noises coming from her now would cause her and her husband to get caught. She stifled the scream that reached the bottom of her throat when her husband pushed a third and then a fourth finger into her ass, driving them all in and out at a now agonizingly slow tempo. She had never been so full before. Until now her husband had only used one finger or his penis to cause her to orgasm. She was so close to cumming now that she wanted to savor the moment of her impending orgasm and tried to pull away from the fingers that were so firmly grinding into her ass. Bereft allowed her to pull away from his fingers and her ass made a loud sucking noise as it reluctantly released the digits from its sheath. Hayley took the moment to spread herself wider and raise her ass higher for easier access, but was unceremoniously flipped over and lifted into the air by her husband.

Bereft smiled sinisterly as Hayley winced and covered her head after hitting the low-hanging ceiling of the cramped shit room. Bereft used only a fraction of the strength that he could take from this body, easily lifting Hayley's full weight by gripping her buttocks and bringing the prize of her barely used vagina to his mouth. The taste was euphoric to him. His enhanced senses allowed him to taste the vestiges of the virgin blood that lingered in her now splayed opening. It was a shame that he had not found the couple the previous day. He would have surely made a day of this one. It was so hard to find virgins that were not of pure soul, for those were the only women that he could enter or taste of himself.

Hayley knew there was something wrong. Although she was enjoying the way her husband was manhandling her, there was something unusual about it. It wasn't what they'd talked about when they were planning this fantasy under the blanket in first class. Her husband did not enjoy performing oral sex and as much as she was enjoying this now, she could not help but feel that Leif just wasn't being himself.

"Uugh, fuck!"

Hayley changed her mind as she felt Leif plunge two fingers back into her ass while never taking his mouth off of her vagina, which was now spewing a surge of fluid from its opening.

The plane shifted to the left, almost throwing Bereft off balance. He could hear the landing gear come down. He righted himself instantly and jammed two more fingers carelessly into Hayley's ass in an attempt to get more of the thick fluids of her body out of her, licking and sucking her pussy ravenously all the while.

Hayley didn't know how much more she could take.

"Leif, Leif, I can't, I can't," she whispered still afraid of getting caught. "I'm cum…cum…cumming."

Bereft did not acknowledge her announcement. Instead he took one hand from under her ass, holding her up with only the four fingers that he had up inside her. The other hand he put around her throat and squeezed. It was a technique he'd taught the Egyptians when civilization was still young. Cutting off the supply of oxygen to the brain during orgasm intensified the experience by a hundred times.

Hayley's eyes bulged from her face. She was bent almost in half with a hand up her ass, a hand around her throat, and her husband's mouth glued to her cunt. She was cumming harder than she ever had in her life and she was dying. Hayley looked down into her husband's eyes but the eyes that looked back were not his own. The eyes were evil, dead, or insane; maybe all of the above.

"I wonder where Leif went," she croaked as the darkness took her.

‡‡‡

When the seatbelt lights went off, Bereft was seated where the blond couple occupied. Everyone was busying themselves with gathering their belongings and preparing to deplane and did not notice that his spouse was not around. He would leave the plane and find another suitable host as soon was possible.

"Is your wife alright?"

It was the flight attendant who had brought them drinks earlier.

"She's fine. Just getting her hair together."

"I'll just go check to see if she needs any help."

In a split-second decision Bereft took the flight attendant. Leif slumped back into the chair. He was not unconscious, but he looked dazed. The flight attendant went to the front of the cabin and clumsily opened the hatch. Chemah and Michelle were the first ones to deplane. Bereft waited only moments before he followed them off the plane in the guise of the flight attendant. The only two people who would have seen the flight attendant leave were the two whose bodies Bereft recently occupied, and they were in no shape to give witness.

Bereft followed Michelle and Chemah all the way to immigration before an officer stopped him. The flight attendant was taking too long explaining why she did not have her passport and was detained. Bereft took the immigration officer too late and lost sight of the couple. Ten minutes later as he wove in and out of people he touched, he thought he saw them leaving the parking area in a large black vehicle. Bereft made note of the make and model of the car, BMW X5. He looked in the direction they were heading and saw the largest spires and towers that he'd ever seen. He looked into the memory of the body he possessed and heard the words, "New York."

Chapter 6

Margaritaville

Héro was running around her mother's apartment holding on tightly to the new Barbie doll that her mother had taken her to get yesterday at Toys-R-Us. She was quite precocious for a five-year-old and knew exactly what she wanted when she dragged her mother to the large Barbie doll section. Margarita pulled a black Barbie doll off the shelf and Héro refused to take it.

"It's not a real Barbie if she's not white," she argued.

"Don't you want a beautiful doll that looks like Mommy?"

"Not unless you're going to get me two dolls."

Margarita watched Héro closely looking for some semblance of herself in the little girl's face and found none. She looked like her father—sandy-brown hair with curls that Margarita would have to use straws to get herself, green eyes with a hint of gray, and mocha-colored skin that was only a hint darker than her father's. Her features were uncannily like her father's now that she was more than a baby. She looked like a female version of her eleven-year-old brother, Tatsuya. The fact that Margarita was not Tatsuya's mother was a testament of the strength of Chemah's genes.

Margarita missed Tatsuya. Years ago when she and Chemah were married and she was his stepmother, they were very close. Now, five years after she had been convicted of manslaughter for the death of his mother, Tatsuya despised her. Margarita only served three years of her five-year sentence, having used every political connection and favor that was owed her to get out early. In the two years since she was released from prison, this was the first time Chemah had allowed her to keep her daughter for more than a weekend. After two weeks with her daughter she was loath to send her back to her father. Margarita was thoroughly enjoying the experience of being a full-time mother again and just yesterday spoke to her lawyer about the possibility of pursuing full custody. He told her exactly what she already knew: Her conviction of manslaughter along with Chemah's standing as one of the most decorated cops in New York City would not make for a great case. She told him to start the process anyway, knowing how fickle the court system could be.

Margarita looked into the mirror to check her hair and makeup. Her rich brown skin was flawless. She barely used any makeup. Even at the age of thirty-six, her skin held its youthful radiance and tautness. She played with the idea of putting her hair up for a second and then let it fall to cascade about her shoulders. She had never used a straightening comb on her hair. The straightness of it was a birthright coming from her Panamanian forbearers. She didn't tell everyone that she was born of two Panamanian immigrants who barely spoke English. She preferred that everyone thought she was African American. Being fluent in Spanish, unknown to those around her, enabled her to gather intelligence that she would not have gotten otherwise.

"Tatsuya says looking in the mirror all the time is stupid."

"It's not stupid if we want to look our best and want people to like us."

"Tatsuya says it doesn't matter what you look like, only how smart you are."

Margarita didn't bother to answer. The two weeks that Héro spent with her had been filled with "Tatsuya says." They could go on with what "Tatsuya says" for a long time before Héro stopped quoting him. Apparently Tatsuya had a lot to say on every subject.

Margarita smiled as she envisioned little Héro taking notes as Tatsuya, dressed like Malcolm X, stood on a soap box making speeches.

"What's so funny?"

"Nothing, dear."

"Tatsuya says we shouldn't laugh at people when nuthin's funny." Héro pouted, instinctively knowing that she was the butt of her mother's humor.

"Tatsuya's right, honey." Margarita turned and bent down toward her daughter and kissed her on the forehead. "Never laugh at anyone's mistakes."

"Yeah, that's what he says." Héro smiled and skipped away, happy to have brought another convert around to her and her brother's way of thinking.

Margarita heaved a sigh and stood up straight as the intercom buzzed. The doorman announced Chemah and Margarita told him that she would be right down. Chemah refused to come up to the apartment when he had to pick up Héro. She stopped inviting him long ago, knowing how mule-headed he was. He still blamed her for the death of Nairobi, Tatsuya's mother, even though the court had deemed that it was manslaughter—an accident.

When she and Héro stepped off of the elevator, Chemah was sitting in the same black leather chair in the lobby that he always sat in. *Creature of habit,* Margarita thought. Héro ran to her father as Margarita allowed the doorman to take Héro's suitcase from her. After father and daughter exchanged kisses and hugs, Chemah turned to Margarita.

"Was she well behaved?"

"She was perfect. Never a problem. We did all sorts of special things together, didn't we, sweetheart?"

"We did our nails, and went shopping and Mommy got me a Barbie doll for my birthday. See?" Héro showed her father the blonde-haired doll.

Chemah and Margarita exchanged a quick glance. They had previously agreed that they would get Héro dolls that had dark skin because they didn't want her to think that beauty only came in with lighter complexion.

"She's beautiful, honey. What's her name?"

"Barbie, Daddy! Everyone knows that."

"Oh yeah, I forgot," he said, giving Margarita a deadly look.

"She seems to have your taste in that department. Must be genetic."

The remark bit at Chemah, but he tried not to let it show. Tatsuya's mother was white and Margarita always suspected that Chemah would eventually choose Nairobi over her. He decided to bite back.

"Yeah, maybe you're right." He looked her dead in the eyes and then turned and walked, carrying Héro toward the door being held open by the doorman.

Unmoved, Margarita walked behind them. As he crossed the threshold of the doorway Chemah turned again.

"Give Mommy a kiss good-bye," he said, putting Héro back on the ground.

Margarita picked her daughter up and held her tightly, only letting her embrace falter long enough to plant little kisses all over Héro's face. Héro laughed and giggled, loving all of the affection her mother gave her.

Margarita finally put her down and Héro ran the few yards to the open car door where her father waited to put her in the backseat. Héro shouted with glee when she saw her big brother there waiting for her. He didn't make a big show of emotion when she jumped in the backseat and threw her arms around him.

"Alright, alright, sit down," he said as he slid the straps across her body, helping her to fasten the buckle of her car seat.

Chemah closed the car door and got into the driver's seat while Margarita looked on from the doorway of her building.

Tatsuya's eyes met hers for a moment and she waved to him. He didn't wave back, and he didn't take his eyes off her. There was no malice in them, but there was no forgiveness.

Chemah drove off and Margarita went back up to her apartment. Once again, she felt the cutting pangs of guilt-ridden loneliness, a constant companion to mothers living on the periphery of their children's lives.

Chapter 7

Small Favors

Sometimes it is more prudent to retreat than to stay and fight. Michelle was not in the greatest of moods since she came back from Israel. The doctor told her that the operation was a total success and with one more operation, which was scheduled for next month at NYU Medical Center, she may regain her sight. *May regain her sight.* Michelle knew it was the impreciseness of the doctor's statement that was bothering her. *She was going through all this trouble, getting her hopes up, and what if none of this worked?* The stem cells that Dr. Yasmin used in her eyes were illegal here in the States. The FDA had not approved the technology yet and if it were not for Dr. Johanson, whom she trusted with her life, she would not have agreed to be the guinea pig that she now said she felt like. She wasn't taking it out on the kids, but she was giving Chemah "the business," on a silver platter. Michelle had a lot of frustration and anxiety that was released in the form of anger, and Chemah was the main recipient when those floodgates opened. Mostly they were verbal assaults, but this morning, they were sexual. Thank God for small favors.

Chemah woke up drowsily from his sleep and felt his penis, already hard, in her hand. It was about five in the morning. He could see glimpses of the light gray sky through the window. He had to pee—and there was no harder erection than when he had to pee.

"Baby, I gotta pee."

"I know, just give me five minutes."

She didn't even take her panties off. She straddled his hips and pulled her panties to the side. She brought the tip of his erection to her opening and rubbed it up and down her slit, trying to produce some moisture. She didn't bother to wait for any to come from him or her as she held him steady and allowed her full weight to come down on his shaft. Her vagina was hot and moist, but not nearly what it should have been for comfortable lovemaking. Chemah could feel the skin on his penis stretch and pull from the excessive friction. It hurt. His eyes were adjusting to the darkness and he could see that Michelle's teeth were clenched. She was in some pain. Her eyes were still covered with gauze bandages, but he didn't need to see her eyes to tell that she was angry again. Still, he didn't want to admit that she was hurting him.

"Take your time, baby, take it slow."

Her answer to him was to raise herself off of him until just the tip of his penis was still inside of her and to thrust herself back down again as hard as she could.

"Uugh! Uugh! Uugh! Uugh!" she grunted again and again as she pushed herself harder and still harder onto Chemah's rock-hard dick. Chemah felt the moisture start to ooze from her coating his dick and welcomed the satiny feel of it.

"Yeah, baby, just like—mmph."

"Shut up," she said, covering his mouth with her hand, not allowing him to finish his plea for her to continue.

That was a welcomed surprise. Shit, he didn't want to do a whole lot of talking while he was fucking anyway. He only talked with Michelle, because she normally asked him to. To show her that he was with it, he grabbed her by the hips and ground the full length of himself into her. Michelle grabbed both his wrists in her small hands and pulled them off her hips and over his head against the headboard. She held them there as she continued to fuck Chemah hard. Chemah allowed her to continue, knowing that doing or saying anything else would stop the motion of her hips. And that's when she started talking to him.

"You like that, don't you? Uugh! Don't you? Uugh! Uugh! Come on, motherfucka, tell me you like it. Tell me you like it. Uugh! Uugh! Uugh! Uugh!"

Chemah didn't know what his role was anymore and didn't care. If the lady he loved needed to make love to him like this, then it was all good. He knew she was a little crazy, but that's what made their world go around.

"Aaaaaaaaaarraaargh!" Michelle screamed into Chemah's face as she convulsed long and hard over his body.

He didn't come, but neither did he feel the need to. It felt good knowing he could be there when she needed him. Michelle didn't say anything as she slumped over his body, with his rock-hard penis still in her. Two full minutes later she rolled off of him and back onto her side of the bed.

Damn, I got the wet spot. Chemah felt the moisture under his ass. He got up out of the bed and walked to the bathroom to pee. He was still hard and bit his lip to focus on his aim after the first stream hit the toilet seat.

"Pull the seat up. You're wetting up the whole damn bathroom," Michelle grumbled from the next room.

Chemah ignored her. He defied her to show that he was still the man of the house. Later that morning, he cursed out loud as he sat on the wet toilet seat to perform his morning evacuation. He heard Michelle laughing in bed.

He was glad to be on his way to work now. He loved his family, but sometimes he needed a good murder to clear his head.

Chapter 8

Work

"What can I do for you, Detective?"

Chemah and his new boss were always very formal with each other. It started when Chemah was forced to make a call to a chief downtown after the newly assigned captain tried to force him to take a partner. Captain Edwin Brea was a no-nonsense, by-the-book-person, having come from a strong male-domineered household. He was Dominican and proud of it as he displayed a small Dominican flag next to the American one on his desk. He had a military background where you always followed rank structure. He didn't put up with insubordination, he was a team player, and he didn't appreciate Chemah's cowboyish ways. Chemah didn't usually go against the rank structure, but after the drama that he'd had with his previous partner, he didn't feel he was ready for another one anytime soon. Captain Brea forced his hand when he tried to partner him with a newly made detective. For the first time since becoming a cop, Chemah called in a favor. The captain received a call the next day "strongly advising" him to rescind his order to Chemah. There was bad blood between them from that day forward.

"My first day back, sir. Just wanted to check in, see if there were any cases that you wanted me to work on."

"You finish all the paperwork on the cases that you finished before you left?" The captain looked back down at the paperwork on his desk.

"Yes, sir, I squared all that away before I went on vacation."

Captain Brea looked up from his paperwork.

"Aren't you back from your vacation a little early?" The captain looked at the detective schedule on the EZ whiteboard behind him. "You're not supposed to be back for another seven days."

"Yeah, I know, but I wasn't doing anything at the house and I thought I'd come back and help out wherever I can."

Captain Brea didn't bother to hide his scorn.

"What do you think, Rivers? The place can't run without you? You think you're the only one that can solve crimes around here? Let me tell you something..."

Shit, I gotta hear this crap again.

"This place was running before you got here and it's going to run whether you're here or not. You do not make, nor break, this unit, do you understand me?"

He didn't wait for Chemah to answer.

"Now get out of here. Take your ass home and don't come back for seven days."

Chemah didn't like it, but the man was in charge and after a few run-ins with Ed Brea, he knew better than to try to persuade him to change his mind. He walked out of the captain's office and could feel the captain's eyes following him all the way back to his desk. Chemah gathered some of his belongings and started for the door. He half-smiled and turned toward the window to the captain's office. The captain's eyes were still on him. Chemah nodded and the captain nodded back, not giving an inch. Chemah knew the captain was not at fault for the way their working relationship was going. Everyone knew that Chemah had made the phone call downtown and it made the captain look bad. Now he was forced to establish that he was still in charge to the rest of the uniformed staff. Sooner or later, Chemah would have to find a way to make up with the captain. He never had a bad relationship with anyone whom he worked with, or for, before now and he wasn't about to allow this one to start a precedent.

Chemah reached the bottom step of the precinct entrance and noticed he was hungry as the smell of sauerkraut and spicy onions wafted toward him from the hot dog stand directly across the street. Chemah crossed against the moving traffic, making a beeline for the stand. At precisely the same time that he was crossing, Chemah noticed a frail old woman jump up from the bench that she was sitting on ten or twelve feet away from the hot dog vendor and run directly to the man serving up franks. From the looks of the lady Chemah never would have thought she had the energy to move that fast. Chemah imagined that the lady was trying to beat him to the stand. Before he could reach the other side of the street the old lady had already reached the stand and before he knew it, was making her way slowly back to the bench where she had started.

Crazy old lady, Chemah thought sympathetically as he reached the other side of the street and saw the lady lie down on the bench, garnering stares from other people who were passing along the way. Chemah reached the hot dog stand at the same time as his old friend Sergeant John Betances, who was coming from the other direction alongside a young female officer.

"Hey, hey, hey, what's going on there? Racing traffic for one of these pimp steaks."

Chemah and the sergeant shook hands and hugged affectionately. They were classmates in the academy together and with cops, that went a long way. Chemah and the sergeant talked for a few moments before they both noticed that the hot dog vendor was waiting patiently. Chemah allowed Sergeant Betances to order first.

"Let me have two grape sodas and four hot dogs with everything."

As an afterthought he looked at the rookie officer who stood behind him and asked, "You want something?"

"Just a Coke, Sarge."

"And a Coke for the new jack," the sergeant said, turning back to Chemah.

"You have a new partner?" Chemah said, eyeing the young female officer who tried to blend into the background.

"Jesus, where are my manners? Come here, kid."

Chemah noticed that the young officer was beautiful, though she was doing her best to tone it down. She wore no makeup and her long satiny hair peeked out in wisps beneath her uniform hat, but there was no way to hide the large breasts, flared hips and seductive eyes of a Latin beauty.

"Detective Rivers, this is Probationary Officer Suarez. Suarez, this is Detective Chemah Rivers. The best damn cop on the job."

Chemah extended his hand to shake with the officer and she saluted him instead.

"Didn't they teach you rooks anything in the academy? You don't salute detectives. They have the same rank as you!"

Chemah and the sergeant shared knowing smiles remembering how they had both made the same mistake once.

"Sorry, sir."

The young officer extended her hand and Chemah took it. Officer Suarez shook hands vigorously and Chemah realized that she was overcompensating because of her beauty. He let go of her hand and smiled down at her.

"That's fine, officer. You're going to be alright. Just follow what Sergeant Betances tells you and you'll go far."

Sergeant Betances beamed at Chemah's dual praise.

"Detective Rivers and I go way back. We started at the academy together," the sergeant said as if that only should earn him an award. "The only recruit to ever take on the whole training staff and come out in one piece—this guy right here." The sergeant gestured with his thumb toward Chemah.

Chemah almost blushed. He had lost count of how many times this story was told in front of him.

"Is that true, sir? You were the recruit that took on ten physical training instructors?"

"You've heard the story?"

"Yes, sir. It's a story that the physical training instructors use to intimidate new recruits. You know? The 'I dare you to try it' tactic. Excuse me for saying it, sir, but we all thought it was bullshit."

Chemah liked the balls on this young lady.

"Bullshit! I was there. It was no bullshit, Suarez. This guy here—"

Chemah put a hand on Sergeant Betances' shoulder, stopping him in mid-sentence.

"You're right, officer. It is bullshit. If memory serves me right, there were only five training instructors there and all I did was make sure I didn't get hurt."

The moment of silence punctuated the embarrassment for everyone.

"Hey, Suarez, I left my wallet in my locker. Pay for the food and park the car. I'll meet you in the stationhouse."

It was a hazing ritual, tricking rookies into paying for the sergeant's food.

"I've got it."

Chemah reached for his wallet, but Suarez already had her money out. She paid for the food. Chemah looked sternly at the Russian immigrant who ran the stand. The vendor lingered a little too long holding onto Officer Suarez' hand when they exchanged money, much longer than should have been comfortable for her. Chemah stared at the man, trying to gauge if he was high. The Russian man looked back at Chemah as if he were seeing him for the first time.

"I'm sorry about that, Chemah. These kids coming out of the academy think they know it all now," Betances offered.

Chemah waved off the apology and looked down the street after Officer Suarez. Chemah willed her to turn around and she did at that precise moment. She seemed, however, to be smirking more than smiling. Even from a distance, Chemah could swear that this was not the first time he had seen those eyes.

Chapter 9

Hell Up In Harlem

Squatty! Squatty! Bereft was heralded as he passed through neighborhoods that were teeming with drugs, alcohol, and the other vices of weak men. What he saw made him long to bring back the days of Sodom. *This place, yes, this place would be a glorious place to start.* The police van Bereft drove attracted the attention of everyone it passed. The drug dealers who preyed on the weak-minded wanted to avoid him. The weak-minded did not want to be disturbed from their search for self-destruction, and the good people, who far outnumbered the other two groups, waited for Bereft or whoever they thought was in the vehicle he drove to put an end to the other two. If there was a guise to keep that would affect these people and convince them to go in the direction that forged Sodom, it was the one that they saw when they saw this vehicle. He would have to think on it, as he was unsure why this visage did not have the same effect on the people who lived in the lower part of the city.

The first man he possessed after three thousand years in bondage was the man who released him. The man was operating the giant crane that was being used to excavate the Dead Sea when he inadvertently unearthed Bereft. That was the first time he'd driven any motorized vehicle. They thought the man had gone mad when he lost control of the vehicle, killing ten people before they were able to subdue him. Alas, it was only

Bereft, at first confused by his surroundings and the new understanding of the miracles this mind that he controlled unlocked for him and then just killing for the fun of it. That was how he'd learned to drive—killing anyone who stood in his way. That quickly became ill advised, as every time he did it he would have to jump into a new body. It seemed that there were laws against driving in such a way and great numbers gathered to try to capture him whenever he did it. He'd lost the use of some very good bodies in this manner and now, though he drove less than cautiously, gleaning a little power and fun from scaring people in his way, he was not driving recklessly enough to draw attention. No one seemed to notice the fun that he was having in the car except the errant person or two who crossed his path. Those he ran off the street, and that took most of the fun out of it for him. In Israel this type of driving would have raised too much suspicion. He had only driven twice in the whole time he was there, preferring to be on the street where he could change bodies at random. There was a term that he got from the mind of this woman that seemed to fit: *upgrading.*

Following Chemah this far north in the city had been very easy, but he lost him at a corner where Bereft was compelled to stop when he saw a child of no more than fifteen years beating an elderly man with only his hands, as others looked on and did nothing. If he had a heart, he would have said that the sight brought a joy to it that was almost overwhelming. Nowhere else, neither in Israel nor Iraq, had he come across such brazen hedonistic behavior. In those places acts of violence from someone so young were always connected to a religious belief, and being so tainted were of no use to Bereft. From the act that he witnessed on the street corner he gained power and gratification without having to cause any of the fear himself. It was at that moment that he decided he could make this his home. Make a new Sodom and rule the city that had previously eluded him.

After riding around for hours Bereft gave up hope of finding Chemah. He would have to find a way for Chemah to come to him again. The woman whom he inhabited was the key. Bereft had not mistaken how Chemah had looked at Suarez as he watched from the body of the sausage meat vendor. He remembered how affectionate Chemah was toward Michelle on the plane and sensed his emotional vulnerability was achieved through physical touch. Even having the light of God shining in you did not make you immune to the sins of the flesh. However, the light of God prevented Bereft from taking Chemah's body through the method of casual contact as used on other victims. Chemah would have to willingly submit his body and desire to become one with Bereft.

It was already two in the morning when Bereft found the circumstances that he was looking for—the chance to do something so heinous that Chemah could not ignore it.

There were four youthful men standing in front of a building marked *Sangre Grande* or Big Blood. It was French. What it meant to the architect who'd placed it there no one in the area could say. Bereft thought it was fitting.

They were life destroyers and poison peddlers, Bereft knew. Normally he would take a group like this as followers and disciples. Ultimately all disciples were to be sacrificed, but these would be sacrificed before they knew the true meaning of hedonism.

Bereft pulled the car up to the front of the building. None of the young men made a move to leave. Bereft got out of the van, leaving it double-parked next to a gray four-door Maxima. He walked slowly toward the men, allowing the hips of the woman he possessed to sway like a reed in a strong wind. The young men all showed their appreciation by grabbing their genitals and holding them as they leaned back in their postures.

The leader of the group showed himself by leaning farther back than the rest.

"You lose something, Officer?" the smallest of them said, gripping himself harder in an invitation for the beautiful female in front of him to take a good look at his package. Bereft didn't bother answering him. He sauntered over to the man he knew was in charge and stood in front of him.

"You are the one in charge?" Bereft allowed his voice to become seductive and sultry.

"In charge? Nah, ain't nobody in charge here. We jus laxin', na'mean?"

"Your product is in this building?"

"Get out my face, bitch! We ain't got nothin' on us."

The leader was starting to sweat. He looked up and down the block, expecting more squad cars to come from both ends of the street any time now.

A cross look came across the beautiful officer's face and she gave the men an order.

"All of you step inside!"

Now all of the men were looking up and down the block. *This bitch had to be crazy coming up here by herself trying to make a drug bust.*

Bereft didn't wait for anyone to move or answer him again. He grabbed the leader of the group by the throat and threw him the few feet to the building steps. The other three men stood quickly at attention, taking positions that made it possible for them to attack her from all sides at their boss's command or run at the first sign of another cop car.

The leader held up a hand, stopping his boys from making any sudden movement. There must be other cars coming and he didn't want to be part of an Abner Louima special.

"You got it, Officer, you got it."

He got up and walked into the building. The other men followed suit, taking their cue from their boss. The last man looked closely at the nameplate on the officer's chest. *Suarez.* He wasn't going to forget it.

Inside of the building all of the men took the same position. They put both hands on the wall and spread their legs.

These fools must think that this body possesses a cock. They're all readying themselves to get fucked.

Without speaking the entity inside of Suarez made its way down the row of men. It felt its way up and down the body of each man the way it saw it should do inside the memory of the beautiful Puerto Rican woman. With each man she lingered a little longer on the crotch, measuring what length and girth each might have.

"All of you turn around!"

"Ah man! What the fuck?"

Only one man said it, but the three hoodlums each thought it. *They ain't got no drugs so they tryna set us up for rapin' a cop.*

"Do you like these?"

The beautiful officer stepped forward, holding a swollen mound of tit flesh in each hand. The way she held them made the areola spread wider, making them bigger than a silver-dollar pancake. The nipple was tiny and surrounded by little bumps that told that she was not faking arousal. It was an offering to the men who stood slack jawed in front of her. They were all waiting for the other cops to come busting in, but no one ever came. The tallest one, Ace, stepped forward.

"Hell yeah! I like those tits."

He grabbed one mound in his large brown hand, kneading it roughly as he pushed Suarez against the wall.

"Is this what you want, bitch?" He grabbed her by the throat.

"No, this is what I want, bitch."

The strength that the officer used to grab Ace by the throat and push him back against the opposite wall scared the shit out of him.

"All of you take your cocks out!"

Her voice did not match the strength that she wielded as she spoke with a gentleness that made them want to do her bidding.

"I'm going to suck your dicks until I get my fill of seed."

When none of them moved, Suarez let go of Ace's neck and took hold of the waistband of his jeans. She stared into his eyes, keeping him still with something akin to fear and a perverse sense of wonder. It didn't take much to tug the denim down around his knees as he wore no belt and his pants already hung beneath his buttocks. The boxer shorts he wore were of no consequence as his penis was already poking through the hole in them. Suarez made a guttural noise in the back of her throat when she saw the thickness of his protrusion. It was only six inches long but it was as thick as the man's own wrist. She knelt in front of him and pushed into his abdomen, causing his head to bang against the wall as she used inhuman strength to maintain that being on her knees did not mean that she was not still in charge. Officer Suarez' lips ovaled and then stretched wide as the thickness of the man's organ expanded even more upon entering the warm and wet cavern that was her mouth.

Ace was afraid to move, but his penis still performed. His boys were watching. They were smiling now. They thought they had finally gotten lucky. The Puerto Rican policewoman was swallowing dick like she was born to do it. She had no problem getting the monster thickness into her mouth and now she had taken it so far down her throat that her lips were pressed against Ace's pubic bone. She gripped his buttocks with both hands and started to pull him out of her mouth. When little more than the head was still in her mouth, she gripped his ass again and pushed him even farther into the back of her throat.

When she pulled him out of her mouth again she gave an order to the other men.

"Pull your cocks out. Now!!!"

If they had any reservations the raw conviction in her last word drained it from them. The remaining three men dropped their pants and waited for what was to come next. They watched as Suarez' cheeks caved in to forcefully suck the last drop of sperm from the now wilting penis that dangled from her mouth. They each inched closer, hoping to be the next one in line.

Suarez licked her now swollen lips, erasing the creamy white evidence that someone had just finished in her mouth. She pushed Ace to the side, watching him trip over the pants that tangled around his ankles. A deadly glare from her convinced him that getting up was not an option as his boys inched forward again. One by one Suarez ravenously devoured the essence of each man. When she had finished sucking off the last one, she turned to Ace again, this time crawling over her most recent victims to get to him.

The fear in Ace's eyes was intoxicating to Bereft. He had no need to climax himself, but knew that he would when he took each of their lives. Four shots rang out in the halls of the building. No one heard the low moans that accompanied each shot.

Mrs. Washington from the fourth floor was the one who had found the bodies at seven o'clock in the morning. She told her neighbors later that day that the bodies were made to form the letter T, and rumor spread that Big Tony, the second biggest drug dealer uptown, was taking over the block. Mrs. Washington answered the questions that the two detectives assigned to the case asked and then they asked her to stick around in case they had more questions later. The detectives knocked on every door in the building, but got no other useful information. It was no surprise that everyone was home to answer the door at nine o'clock in the morning. Mrs. Washington was the only person in the whole building who had a job to get to and she never even made it to work.

Chapter 10

Who's Watching You?

Chemah answered the phone on the second ring. Michelle was still in the shower and he heard her curse when she heard the phone ring.

"Damn!"

"I've got it, Chelle."

"If it's Tanya, tell her I'm washing my hair and I'll call her back as soon as I'm finished."

"Hello, Rivers residence."

"This is Captain Brea. Detective Rivers?"

"Yes, sir."

"I need to see you in my office within the hour."

"Is it important, sir? After our talk yesterday, I made plans with my wife to take her—"

"I wouldn't call you otherwise, Detective. One hour."

Chemah stared at the receiver. He couldn't believe his bad luck. He put the receiver down slowly, thinking of an angle to soften Michelle up. He walked toward the open bathroom door.

"Uh, baby?"

"Sounds like you're in some sort of trouble with that asshole captain."

"Nah, we spoke yesterday. He would have told me if anything was wrong."

"You know, for someone who solves as many crimes as you do, you're really not that good at judging character."

Chemah chuckled.

"No, I mean it. Once you want to like a person, you put the blinders on. You couldn't tell me if any of your friends were up to no good."

"That's just because I don't have many friends."

Chemah pulled back the shower curtain and reached in to grab a handful of Michelle's ass. Michelle allowed him a quick feel and splashed water at him over her shoulder. Chemah closed the curtain again.

"We can still have dinner later tonight."

"That's cool. I'll call you if Tanya and I decide to go out instead. I called Mrs. Richmond. She's still picking up the kids after school today. She says I haven't gotten enough rest since my operation. What do you think?"

"We just got back two days ago. She's probably right. Maybe we can go away for a couple of days for a real vacation."

Chemah reached behind the curtain again, this time playfully grabbing a breast.

"Stop playing," she said, smacking his hand away.

Michelle turned the water off, pulled back the curtain, and adjusted the goggles that she wore to protect her newly operated eyes from the water.

"Hand me that towel."

Chemah handed her the green towel hanging on the back of the door. She stepped out of the shower and wrapped the towel around her head. Chemah leaned back against the doorframe and watched droplets of water fall from every part of her body onto the slate-covered bathroom floor. Michelle hardly ever used a towel to dry her body unless she was in a rush. Chemah knew she liked to air-dry and he never tired of watching her perfectly proportioned body. The goose pimples were now starting to show everywhere on her and both her nipples were raised a full inch away from her breasts.

"Do you think I could have some privacy now?" she asked with a gregarious smile as she turned in the general direction of Chemah's breathing.

"Damn. Can't I watch a little longer?'

"Not if you're going to make it downtown, you can't."

"Hmm. I almost forgot."

Chemah took two steps toward her and planted a kiss on her neck.

"Ooh, baby, brush your teeth before you go. Your breath smells like a bum's pocket."

Chemah pulled away from her.

"Why do you always have to make jokes?"

"Baby, I'm serious. Your breath smells like you had shit-flavored Life Savers."

Chemah was used to this. She was always practicing her comedy routine and he was usually the focus of it. She was on a roll and he knew she wouldn't stop until he was gone.

"Alright, I'm leaving."

"Smells like the Tidy Bowl Man stepped in shit and decided to go for a walk in your mouth. Baby, just brush your teeth, you don't have to leave yet."

Chemah was at the bottom of the steps and could still hear her.

"Breath smellin' like cheese doodles. Light on the cheese, heavy on the doodoo—"

Chemah closed the door. He was glad that he couldn't hear her anymore.

‡‡‡

The door to the captain's office was open, so Chemah walked in without announcing himself. Ed Brea was pacing the floor and stopped to look at his watch when Chemah came through the door. It irked him that Chemah made it to his office in the allotted time that he gave him. It was one less thing that he could call him on. Chemah looked at his own watch: 10:30 a.m. He made it downtown in thirty-five minutes. He was a loner, but he prided himself on being able to follow orders too. He wanted to show Captain Brea that despite their earlier misgivings about each other, he was still a team player.

Captain Brea sat behind his desk again. Despite the calm image that he attempted to project, Chemah could see two arteries pulsing on the side of his neck. Captain Brea couldn't be any more than four, maybe five, years older than Chemah and yet the sprinkle of gray in his hair made him look at least ten years older. Chemah had seen him spend late hours in the office, each time eating mounds of greasy Chinese takeout. Chemah tried not to stare at the pulsating arteries and found himself concerned about the man's health. Maybe he was on high blood pressure medication.

"Is everything alright, sir?"

Captain Brea looked pissed.

"Is everything alright? Is everything alright, you ask? Shut that goddamn door."

Chemah reached behind himself to close the door, but kept his eyes on the captain. He wasn't used to anyone besides Michelle using this tone of voice with him, but he kept his head, determined not to lose his composure.

"I got a call from the FBI field office this morning because they're now taking over a murder case from the air marshals. They went over the plane's manifesto trying to gather witnesses for a murder that they believe happened over international waters. And guess whose name was the first one on the list?"

Chemah's eyes went wide.

"That's right, yours."

Chemah didn't open his mouth. He didn't want to interrupt the captain, preventing him from disclosing any information that he could use to defend himself.

"Not only were you on the plane, but according to the manifesto, you were seated in front of the victim in first class."

Chemah allowed his eyebrows to come down and he quieted his breathing, trying to concentrate as the captain continued his tirade. His mind brought up the image he was looking for.

Directly behind me, blonde woman, blond man. Blue eyes. Maybe Norwegian, German, or Scandinavian. Behind me to the left, Jewish businessman, black hair, short, sickly.

The images of the beginning of the flight were clear to him, but he had been too intent on getting Michelle home when the flight landed and hadn't been paying attention to much else.

The couple had been giggling and laughing most of the flight. Chemah had to guess it was the businessman who'd died. *He did look sickly. Maybe the air marshals were mistaken about the cause of death.*

"Then I get a call from the commissioner's office saying that we have to do our own investigation into the case because some diplomat's kid is involved."

"I'll get right over there and start the investigation."

"You're not assigned to the case."

Chemah waited for an explanation, but none came.

"So how did he die?"

"How did who die?"

"The Jewish business-looking guy from first class?"

Captain Brea got up from his seat slowly and came from behind his desk. He stopped in front of Chemah with arms folded across his chest.

"How do you know about the Jewish businessman?"

Chemah wanted to remain respectful to the captain, but he was growing tired of his ineptness. Maybe if he were less formal the captain would relax a little.

"Cap, you just told me that this man was murdered."

The captain bit his tongue. He wanted to tell Chemah that he didn't like being called "Cap." He liked to hear the full title of captain whenever he was addressed.

"I said that someone in first class was murdered. You just said the Jewish businessman was dead. How did you know?"

"So he was the one that was murdered?"

Captain Brea waited with arms folded—waiting to hear Chemah say anything that he could use against him.

"Are you saying that everyone who was on that plane and in first class are dead except me and my wife?"

Chemah waited for Captain Brea to answer, but Captain Brea seemed to be waiting for something else. Chemah refused to ask or say anything else, realizing that the man was either being obstinate or was trying to trip him up. Chemah had nothing to hide, but he thought his own silence would be a better tactic at this time. The staring contest only lasted about forty-five seconds but it felt eerily longer to Captain Brea, who saw no emotion at all when he stared into Chemah's grayish-green eyes. Hiding intentions or emotions was an acquired skill from years of studying the martial arts. It was second nature to Chemah.

"So you're saying you don't know anything about the murder on the plane."

"No, sir."

"And nothing about the Jewish businessman who sat behind you for twelve hours."

This time Chemah didn't even open his mouth. He simply shook his head no. The captain stared at Chemah hard again, trying to gain an edge, but again was forced to turn away, seeing only death in his eyes. The captain went behind his desk again and sat down.

"Alright, Detective. Have a seat and I'll fill you in before you go talk to the feds."

Chemah took the seat in front of Captain Brea's desk and allowed himself to relax a little. Captain Brea opened up the top drawer of his desk and took out a pack of gum. He offered Chemah a stick and Chemah held up a hand, declining the offer.

"Tryin' to quit the cigarettes, this seems to be the only thing that helps."

The captain unwrapped a stick for himself, popped it into his mouth, and chewed a few times before he started to speak.

"Do you remember the couple who sat behind you in first class?"

Chemah nodded and folded his hands in his lap, intent on listening closely to every detail.

"Well, they decided they were going to join the mile-high club on that plane from Israel to New York. It appears that they were into some rough sex. The FBI forensic team says they must have been going at it pretty hard before the husband started to asphyxiate his wife. They believe the asphyxiation was part of the sex too, and normally would be calling it manslaughter."

Chemah nodded his understanding, having investigated many cases where he had determined that the cause of death was accidental death by asphyxiation during a sexual act.

"But that's where it goes goofy. After the woman dies in the bathroom the guy must have gone crazy. He must have started to really beat on the corpse, because they say that the woman has about twenty broken bones. It's a total mess. They've got the guy under observation down at Bellevue Hospital and they aren't letting anyone near. I assigned detectives Rodriguez and Flores to the case last night and they're being dicked around. I talked to a Special Agent Morris this morning down at the bureau and he just gave me the runaround. We'll have to wait until they're finished so that we can get a crack at him."

Okay, it's the wife who died, but what happened to the Jewish businessman?

"The other guy who sat behind you died of a stroke in a toilet at the airport. Nobody realized that the two were related until they tried to find everyone who was on the plane that day. No foul play was suspected. The guy was taking a shit and probably pushed too hard. His brain started leaking, and his heart was already overextended, according to the coroner, and he expired."

"So we're not investigating the death of the businessman. What was his name?"

The captain looked at a Post-it note on his desk.

"Schlomo, Schlomo Horowitz."

"So we're not looking into the death of Schlomo Horowitz."

"No, we're not. The guy's body was flown back to Israel yesterday. As far as I know he's already in the ground—Jewish custom and all that. Anyway, it's like I said, the coroner said he died of natural causes." The captain eyed Chemah for a reaction. He'd heard many stories about Chemah before he got to this precinct. Stories about how Chemah always found what he was looking for, and how he always knew things that no one else did. Captain Brea had solved his share of cases when he was a detective, but he never received the acclaim that he thought he should. He solved his cases using proven police techniques, not gut instincts or any other bullshit insight everyone claimed Chemah had. "Unless you want to say something different," he added.

Chemah shook his head no to the captain, but thought about the odds of two people dying from the same flight on the same day. The chances would be as great as hitting the winning numbers in the lottery—too much of a coincidence.

"You said the feds called you. Would that be Special Agent Sidney Morris?"

"You know him?"

"We worked a few cases together a couple of years back. Good guy. He's by the book, but he likes to work out problems. If he didn't let Rodriguez or Flores in it means he's working on something big. I have his number at my desk. I'll give him a call right now."

Chemah got up from his chair and walked out of the room.

The captain started to sweat. If Chemah knew this FBI agent well he would find out that they had asked for him to come out as the NYPD representative for the case. The captain had refused and told them that Chemah wasn't available. Special Agent Morris insisted that they still had to talk to him as a matter of course, as one of the probable witnesses on the flight. When the captain realized he wouldn't be able to keep Chemah from having even this small part in this case that eventually would be internationally publicized, he relented and told Agent Morris that he would have Chemah come in.

The captain looked out of the window that separated his office from the bullpen of cubicles outside. Chemah's cubicle was out front and not concealed from his view. He could see Chemah talking on the phone animatedly as with a long-time friend and hated the feeling of jealousy and resentment that welled up in him. This afternoon when Chemah returned from being interviewed by the FBI, the captain would insist that he go back home and finish his vacation. Captain Brea looked at the paperwork that was still unfinished on his desk and almost wished he were back on the streets.

Five minutes later Chemah knocked on Edwin Brea's office door again. The captain waved Chemah in and stopped the work he was doing.

"I'm on my way down to FBI headquarters to talk to Special Agent Morris. It should be a quick interview. They say it's pretty cut-and-dried. The husband isn't talking, but they've got all the evidence they'll need already. I shouldn't be more than a couple of hours."

"Alright, come see me when you get back."

Chemah feigned leaving the office and then turned back to the captain. "Oh yeah, and I got Agent Morris to let Rodriguez and Flores talk to the perp, but he'll only consent to them doing an interview if I'm there walking the guys through."

Edwin Brea glared at Chemah.

Chemah shrugged his shoulders. "I don't know why, Cap. I guess the guy trusts me."

Now he was fucking with the captain and the captain knew it.

He would have to share this moment with Michelle. Just this morning she had told him how he couldn't judge the character of people that he liked. Well, he had tried to like Captain Edwin Brea, but after the phone conversation that he'd just had with his man down at the bureau he knew it would never happen. When Special Agent Morris had called Brea and asked for Chemah and accounted to the captain that Chemah had been on a flight where a murder occurred, the captain had taken the liberty of slighting him and slandering his name. "I knew this guy was a fraud. I was going to have him under review when he got back anyway," he'd confided in Special Agent Morris before he knew the complete nature of the inquiry.

"It was a bitch move, Chemah, but with guys like this you have to really watch your back. He's a loose cannon," his good friend Agent Morris had warned him.

If Chemah followed the philosophies of *The Art of War*, as he usually did, he would have been thinking, *Keep your friends close, keep your enemies closer.* Today he was thinking, *I'm tired of kissing this guy's ass anyway.*

Chemah eyed the manila envelope on the captain's desk.

"Are those the pictures of the victim from the airplane that Agent Morris sent for Rodriquez and Flores to look at?"

Chemah reached for them, but before he could get them the captain put his hand over the envelope.

"I told you, it's not your case."

"I know, Cap." Chemah tried sounding put off. "But I promised Agent Morris I would have a look at the pictures before I got there so that Detectives Rodriguez and Flores wouldn't have to bother them with any unnecessary questions. They know I have an extensive background in forensics."

The captain took his hand off the envelope and Chemah slid it off the desk and put it under his arm.

"Thanks, Cap, I'll let you know how things go."

He walked out of the office knowing full well that he would not tell the captain anything unless he was forced. Rodriguez and Flores would no doubt let the captain know all of the particulars. He was cool with them. They didn't have a problem with Brea and he wouldn't make it a problem for them.

He walked over to where they sat and gave them the details that the FBI agent had shared with him. They didn't mind that Chemah would be coming with them to do the interview. Although he didn't hold the rank, in the last couple of years they had been without a lieutenant and being the senior detective, the previous captain forced Chemah to assume some of that leadership role. Captain Brea had taken all of those responsibilities away from Chemah, but a lot of the detectives still looked to him for direction.

After they were briefed Chemah told them where to meet him behind Bellevue Hospital. He would be driving his own car. Even though the case already piqued his interest, he had no intention of trying to take it over. His boy at the bureau had told him it was a done deal and all but a closed case. The NYPD detectives who were put on the case could follow the FBI notes and write a closing investigation with no problem. After the talk he'd had with Agent Morris over the phone, the only reason to even come down to see Leif Shultz in Bellevue's lockdown was to get his mind off of the stress at home. He loved Michelle, but she was taking out her anxieties about regaining her sight on him and it was wearing him down. She had been easier to live with when she thought she'd never see again.

Chemah rushed out of the precinct only moments before the media descended upon it. Another officer was being indicted for using excessive force. If Chemah had known about it, he would have stayed to support the officer. Later he would be surprised to find that it was the beautiful Puerto Rican officer, Suarez, that he met yesterday.

Chemah sped off still thinking about having dinner later with Michelle. The thought of her still stressing about her operation was not appealing to him. He felt himself tensing again when the manila folder caught his eye on the passenger seat. He reached out for it, thinking that the pictures would get his mind off of his home life. Chemah stopped at a traffic light and opened the manila envelope. Cars were honking their horns and drivers were cursing Chemah through their open windows as they passed for more than two minutes before Chemah reacted.

Chemah pulled his car over to the side of Seventy-Second Street and York Avenue and went over each picture in the envelope over and over again. There was no mistaking it. He could see the formation of the broken bones. There was no mistaking a cross—upside-down or not.

Chapter 11

How Low Can You Go?

Base greeted Chemah at the door. He was an immense dog—his purple tongue indicated Chow—but for all anyone else knew he could have really been part bear given his size and ferocity. He was always waiting by the door and always looked disappointed when a family member came in, rather than some stranger for him to bite. He was a good seeing-eye dog, but if anybody got too close to Michelle, Base was sure to lunge. Michelle was usually able to tell when he was going to attack and would pull him back at the right time. Sometimes she wasn't fast enough and many people had been bitten. So far no one had the gall to pursue a lawsuit against a blind woman and her seeing-eye dog.

Chemah patted the dog on the head and headed upstairs. The children weren't in their rooms, which meant that he wouldn't find Michelle in the bedroom either. She would have called Mrs. Richmond and had her bring the children home if she were in the house.

Chemah heard the door slam downstairs and he could clearly make out the voices of two females in the living room.

"Aaaaaaaaaaaagh!"

"No, Base, down!"

One of them was definitely Michelle, but he couldn't tell at first whom the scream came from. Chemah checked his watch and couldn't believe it was already two-thirty in the morning. He made his way downstairs and found Michelle still giggling as she held Base's collar. Base was still trying to get at Rhonda, Michelle's best friend, but Michelle knew better than to let him go.

"Get him out of here, Michelle. That dog is the devil."

Rhonda was holding the back of her leg, her skirt was lifted above her thigh, and she was checking for blood.

"Did he break the skin?" Chemah asked as he approached Michelle still holding Base. Michelle let Chemah take Base from her and Base settled down in his hands.

Rhonda quickly pushed her skirt down afraid that she had inappropriately exposed herself in front of her best friend's man.

"No, I'm alright," she said hurriedly.

Chemah took Base and led him through the living room and into the kitchen. He let Base go out the back door and into the backyard. When Chemah came back into the living room Michelle was trying to talk Rhonda into spending the night.

"Come on, girl, spend the night. It's got to be late already. What is it, about o' dark-thirty in the morning?"

Chemah noticed that Michelle was slurring her words. Now as she moved forward she tripped over the coffee table. In the two years that they were together Chemah had never seen her trip over anything. If she bumped into anything once she never bumped into it again. Chemah and Rhonda both reached out to grab her as they saw her stagger forward.

"I'll take her upstairs."

Michelle pulled away from Chemah.

"I don't want to go upstairs."

She staggered backward, taking Rhonda with her. They both fell on the new velvet, eggplant-colored couch that Chemah and Michelle had purchased two months earlier. Michelle loved the texture and the color seemed very regal to Chemah. The weight of Rhonda's and Michelle's bodies falling at the same time made the wooden legs groan and Chemah thought he heard a spring pop. *So much for the new couch.*

Rhonda adjusted herself on the couch and pushed Michelle off her.

"I'll stay a while, but you've got to stop acting so stupid. I have never known you to be a sloppy drunk."

Rhonda winked at Chemah.

Michelle instantly propped herself up against the high back of the couch.

"I'm okay, I'm okay. Just stay with me a while. Please."

Rhonda looked to Chemah and he nodded to her, granting his permission.

"Alright, I'll stay, but you can't keep me up talking all night. You're my only friend, but you're not my only client. Saturday is only a day off for normal people. For us in the entertainment business it's the beginning of a work week."

Michelle made a face. "You don't hardly work that hard. If it weren't for me you wouldn't even have a career in entertainment."

"What? Bitch, if it weren't for me, you wouldn't be able to book a gig at a boy's club dinner—"

"I'll leave you two ladies to your discussion. I'm going to bed."

Michelle turned to his voice as if she had forgotten he was ever there.

"Good night, baby."

Rhonda waved to him as he turned back to look at them from the stairs.

Thirty minutes later Chemah heard the pad of footsteps outside his room. The footing was too sure. It definitely wasn't Michelle. Chemah sat up in his bed as Rhonda came to his bedroom doorway.

"I was hoping you were still up."

"Yeah, I've got a lot of work stuff on my mind—can't get to sleep."

"I figured that. You know she called you earlier from the club so that you could pick her up. Your phone went straight to voice mail."

"I was doing an interrogation. I had to turn the phone off. It took longer than I thought."

"You've got to know Michelle's not really feelin' you right now."

"I've been getting that vibe. I don't know what I did wrong. Since the operation, she's been buggin'. As far as she's concerned, I can't do anything right."

"Have you ever thought that maybe she's just afraid of getting her sight back?"

"Why would you think that she's afraid?"

"I'm not psychic, Chemah. She told me she's afraid. I probably shouldn't be telling you any of this, but I'm not just her agent, I'm her best friend. Everything has been going so well for her, between work, the kids, and you. She never thought she'd have it all. And now with the possibility of her getting her sight back, she thinks everything will be different."

Chemah thought about this for a moment.

"You think maybe that's why she's been dogging me?"

"She did a whole skit on you at the club tonight. You should have heard it. She bombed big time. There was nothing funny about it. She just talked about you and your relationship and how you guys always fight."

"I don't fight. She fights."

"That's not how she sees it."

"Fuck how she sees it, that's the way it is. For example, the other night when we were on our way home, I stopped at the drive-through ATM. I pointed out to her that at any time she wanted to use the drive-through ATM, she could because it was equipped with Braille. She began ranting, 'Who the fuck thought up that brilliant fucking idea? Since when do blind people drive?' Then she went off on this tangent about how I didn't really 'get her' and her needs. She was *beasting* at me for the rest of night!"

"No pun intended, but try to see things her way. She's blind and was about as bitter as anyone can be. Along comes a man who accepts who she is. And then all of a sudden she's not that person anymore. She's new, she's vigorous, and she's independent."

"She's independent now."

Rhonda shook her head.

"No, you didn't know Michelle back when she had her sight. She was a whole different person. She was wild. No one could tame her. And here she is now with you, a domesticated cat."

"Is that how she sees herself?"

"That's how she sees it, and she was content with it. But now with the prospect of seeing again she's not so sure."

"Well, if that's how she feels, I'm not trying to hold her back. She can leave any time she wants."

"Don't get your panties in a bunch. Nobody's talking about leaving. She's probably more concerned about whether you'll still want her here."

Chemah was pensive for a moment and realized that he was not being sensitive to the emotional turmoil that Michelle might be going through.

"Anyway, I thought you should know what was going on. I love my girl and I think she deserves to be happy—despite what she thinks about herself. And don't go mentioning that we even had this conversation. She's blind but she'll still whip my ass if she finds out."

Chemah nodded and smiled. He remembered how he once had to hold Michelle back from fighting another parent at Tatsuya's school.

"I'm going to leave now. She's asleep on the couch. When she wakes up tell her to call me."

Rhonda walked back down the hall.

"And you can stop looking at my ass," she called over her shoulder.

Chemah was in fact admiring her ass. He wasn't trying to be disrespectful, it was one of those asses you couldn't help looking at.

Chemah tried to go to sleep again, but kept tossing and turning. After hours of interrogating Leif Schultz he had gotten nowhere. He had all but taken over the investigation from Rodriguez and Flores even though the captain had told him to stay out of it. He was the only one who knew that this murder somehow tied into the murders in Fallujah and

Israel. If the FBI hadn't connected the two yet, he wasn't going to give it to them. In the morning he was going to call Inspector Yankow and find out if any more murders had occurred abroad. After interrogating Leif Schultz he had more questions than he had answers.

Chemah finally fell into a restless sleep around four-thirty. He dreamt of Michelle seeing again, and he dreamt of following a trail of dead bodies. Neither dream made him feel particularly secure.

Chapter 12

Night Life

Margarita's date the previous night had been a debacle. She woke feeling ill if not a bit off-kilter. She got up from her bed and put on her bedroom slippers. A hot shower would be nice, but she needed some coffee first, so she went into the kitchen and put on the coffeemaker.

Margarita turned on the nineteen-inch flat-screen television she had on the countertop to NBC news. The smell of coffee started to pervade the room immediately and Margarita reached for a coffee mug, too anxious to wait for the entire pot to brew. She replaced the pot with the mug and waited for the mug to almost overflow with the piping hot liquid before returning the pot to its rightful place. Two sips of the bitter brew and Margarita felt better. She sucked on the part of her tongue that the coffee had burned, trying to regain some of its sensation, when the voice on the television caught her attention.

"Live at the Thirty-Second Precinct. We are still waiting for word of the police officer who was arrested last night for the murders of four alleged drug dealers. The chief of police entered the building an hour ago and has promised to address the city in a press conference within the next few minutes."

Margarita took another sip of her coffee and almost choked on it when she saw Chemah walk into the precinct behind the newscaster. He still took her breath away. She was surprised that he was even working on a Saturday. She knew he worked odd hours, but he usually liked to be at home when she picked Héro up from the house.

Margarita finished her coffee and headed for the shower. The hot water against her skin combined with the caffeine she consumed was working its magic on her. The events of the previous night washed through her mind and she combed her fingers through her wet hair, untangling the knots that were caused by the sweating she had done. Margarita soaped herself gently between her legs, careful not to arouse herself the way she had before she left the house on her date last night. It was a memory that she wished that she could forget.

‡‡‡

After showering she was extremely aroused. She dressed meticulously. The red Vera Wang evening dress with the plunging neckline was like a secret weapon. Men couldn't stop looking at her when she wore it. Her date came to the door in a gray Hugo Boss suit. Richard Fenton had style and he was gorgeous. He was forty years old, relatively young for a senior partner at Langdon & Langdon, one of the biggest entertainment law firms in Manhattan. Margarita had met him at a fundraising luncheon and they hit it off right away. Dinner was good. They ate at Quixote's on Twenty-Third Street. The paella was an aphrodisiac. They finished the seafood and rice out of the pot and then Richard decided they should have oysters. Margarita knew the effect the oysters would have on her, but she was already feeling sexy and had decided when they first met that she would be giving him the goodies. He seemed to know it too. He was seducing her as much as she was seducing him. They were both dragging out the inevitable outcome of the night for as long as they could.

After dinner they caught a cab back to her place, holding hands the whole way like teenage lovers. Margarita thought it was cute. It had been a long time since she thought about a man the way she was thinking about this one. She couldn't help but compare him to Chemah. The style, the self-confidence, and the beauty were all there. She smiled, thinking that this man had one up on Chemah—he had vision and ambition. Chemah never wanted to be more than a police detective. If it weren't for the million dollars that she had given him when she left him with their daughter, he would probably be penniless right now.

When they reached her apartment Margarita invited Richard up for a drink. He kissed her gently on the mouth and took her hand again as the doorman let them into the building. Inside the apartment Margarita poured them both a drink. Like her, he drank scotch straight. They sat on the couch talking and each minute brought them closer and closer to each other until soon their thighs touched. Richard let his hand caress the softness where her neck and clavicle met. Margarita leaned in to be kissed gently again.

It only took another minute and both she and Richard were enjoying the taste of each other's tongues. They alternately entered each other's mouths, savoring the flavors that they found. Margarita broke their embrace first. She was breathing heavily and didn't want to hold back anymore. She wanted more from him, but she didn't want to cheapen the encounter by doing it in the living room.

Margarita stood up, smoothed out her dress, and took a deep breath.

"Give me ten minutes and then come into the bedroom," she said, pointing down the hall to the master bedroom.

"Are you sure about this? I don't want you to feel pressured. It is our first date and we—"

Margarita put her index finger gently to his lips, instantly quieting him.

"I'm sure. Just give me a few minutes to slip into something more comfortable."

Margarita could already feel herself getting wet as she entered the sanctum of her bedroom. She had felt some of what he had between his legs when he leaned in to kiss her on the couch and she thought it might be impressive.

Anyone who knew Margarita intimately knew one sure thing about her—she loved to go down on men. Some women didn't like to because it made them feel like they were being too submissive but Margarita felt the opposite. She felt as if she were in complete control of a man when she had him in her hands and her mouth. Every man she had ever been with, including her ex-husband, Chemah, believed that they had lucked out when they found out how much she enjoyed performing fellatio. They also found out very quickly afterward that they were the ones who would submit to whatever she wanted when they were with her. She could make a man cry her name out loud and she knew the power of her name. She made men beg her to stop or beg her to continue and she knew as they did that they were her slaves and she their master. When she had a man in her mouth she had their full attention. The whole truth was that she loved sex, but nothing made her cum harder than sucking dick. A pseudo-psychiatrist would have said that she had an oral fixation and they would have been wrong. Margarita had a god complex. She wanted men to worship her and this was the way she got them on their knees to pray and give homage to her.

Margarita wasted no time when she entered her bedroom. She unceremoniously ripped off her clothes, then she turned on the light of her walk-in closet and searched for the piece of negligee that she thought most fitting. She was fond of the Fredrick's collection and had more of their items hanging unused on the far end of the closet than she wanted to admit. She picked an all-white sheer chiffon gown that was held together by nothing more than a satin ribbon around the waist. It was reminiscent of a Roman toga. Margarita started to put the gown on and felt the discomfort of the overflowing moisture in her panties. She quickly peeled them off and thought that maybe she should clean up before putting the gown on, but quickly decided against it. She had no need for panties anyway. She knew her punany was clean otherwise and did not want to wash away the nectar that was seeping out. Nature in its wisdom had seen fit to fill her juices with pheromones that drove most men absolutely crazy. It did not behoove her to tamper with nature.

Margarita put the gown on and tied the bow at the waist. She stepped back into her bedroom and looked into the full-length mirror that was opposite her bed. She was pleased with what she saw. If not for the chocolate smoothness of her skin she could be mistaken for a Greek goddess. Margarita turned and walked to her bed. She played with the light console at her nightstand for a moment, lowering the intensity of the overhead light to give the room a hazy and soft feel. She sat atop the gold comforter on the bed and leaned back against the overstuffed pillows, posing for the mirror in front of her. She wanted to overwhelm Richard with the sight of her the moment he entered the room. She found the position she wanted and waited as still as a statue for another two minutes before she heard Richard coming down the hall. As he came closer to her room, she repositioned herself one last time and then settled back in her pillows, gazing longingly at the door.

Margarita almost lost her composure when Richard came to the doorway. She was immediately sorry she had dimmed the lights so much. Richard was at the doorway totally nude. She knew he was in shape for his age, but *damn.* His body looked to be chiseled from some obsidian marble. Every muscle showed striations that belied his hard work at the gym.

All of that being the truth, it was not what made Margarita gasp. It was what he held in his hand that was the most impressive. Margarita thought that if she had made the room any darker she would have sworn the man was coming into the room riding on a broomstick.

Richard smiled when he saw the look on Margarita's face. He had seen that look on many other women and he knew the sight of his body cut an impressive image and gave him an edge. He came into the room slowly, allowing Margarita to devour the sight of him. He stopped at the foot of her bed and licked his lips as his eyes drank in the sight of her in return.

"My God, you're beautiful."

Margarita became herself again when she heard him utter those words and started to reach toward him.

"No, please don't move. Let me just look at you for a second."

Margarita smiled and allowed herself to relax against the pillows. She felt beautiful in the moment and there was no reason why she couldn't let Richard enjoy her beauty too. He seemed to be enthralled by her. She thought she could see his penis getting even harder in his hand at the sight of her and then she was sure of it when he started to slowly stroke himself as he let his eyes wander up and down her body. Margarita didn't blame him and she was getting turned on watching him play with his dick. She could feel her mouth fill with saliva at the thought of having it in her mouth. She reached to her waist and pulled at the white satin bow that held the gown together. When it was undone the gown fell to either side of Margarita's body, exposing her abundant brown-capped breasts, her flat stomach, and freshly groomed swollen vulva.

There was a sharp intake of breath and Margarita saw Richard grip his dick tighter as if trying to stop a surge of fluid from escaping him. Margarita watched wide-eyed as Richard's dick got even longer and thicker. She estimated it was at least fourteen inches long. She wanted to say a foot, but she had used rulers before and Richard was well beyond a ruler.

"Touch yourself."

"Huh?"

"Touch yourself. You're making me want to come already. I can hardly take it anymore, you look so damn good."

Margarita started to reach out to him again, but he stopped her.

"No, baby, just touch yourself. I can take care of this from here and then I'll take care of you. Just touch your pussy a little. Damn, I can smell that bitch from here."

Margarita was intrigued by his suggestion. The only one whom she had ever let take charge of her during sex had been Chemah and those times had been few and far between. She quickly assessed Richard's request and thought there would be no harm in it for the sake of setting off their relationship in a mutually satisfying way.

Margarita brought her right hand to her left breast and gave the hard nipple a gentle pinch. Her mouth formed an "O" as she let the pleasure pain course a trail from her nipple to her vagina. Margarita's hand followed that trail to her pussy and let her middle finger slide between her soaked cunt lips.

"Shit, that's what I'm talking about, baby. Do it. Fuck yourself for me."

Margarita started to get into it. She was watching Richard stroking his dick while watching her play with her pussy and it was turning her on. She let a second finger dip inside of her and every time she pulled back she would allow the palm of her hand to slide against her protruding clitoris before pressing the two digits back into her clenching pussy. She watched the head of Richard's dick oozing pre-cum and she licked her lips imagining how good it would taste in a few moments. The veins around Richard's dick were pulsating and she felt like a vampire that had to satisfy its thirst.

"Do it, baby, do it," Richard egged her on.

Margarita was damn near in a frenzy, pumping into herself with that dick just a second away from her mouth. She could see that Richard was getting close too and wondered how much longer she would have to endure the maddening exercise in restraint. At the moment she resolved she would have to lunge for Richard's cock because she saw the look on his face that told her it was her time. She would make her move at the precise moment, right before he would cum or cry from wanting to—this was the time when men could least resist her. Time stood still for a moment between Margarita and Richard and for that moment Margarita thought their souls were kindred. Then Richard did the unimaginable. He bent at the waist while continuing to stroke himself and put the head of his cock in his own mouth.

Margarita hurt herself ripping her fingers from her own vagina.

"What the fuck!"

She couldn't get all the words out that she wanted to say and stopping her masturbation didn't deter Richard from his sucking. Margarita saw the veins on his cock jump and Richard's throat convulse as he swallowed his own seed.

That's when Margarita lost it.

"You sick motherfucker!"

Margarita jumped from the bed and reached behind the nightstand. She picked up the bat that she kept there and started swinging. The first hit caught Richard on the shoulder and by surprise as he was still intent on sucking his own dick. The second swing didn't. Richard was quite agile and moved out of the way in time as the bat just missed his head. Margarita swung again, but now Richard was totally clear of her.

"Bitch, are you crazy? You better put that fucking bat away before you hurt somebody."

Margarita was not unfamiliar with his intention. *What he really meant was put that fucking bat away before I hurt you.*

Margarita held the bat high above her head. Her hate was unwavering.

"Get...the fuck out of my house!"

Richard took a step toward Margarita. His limp penis was still dripping cum on the floor and the sight infuriated her. She threw the bat at him and Richard leapt backward to avoid being hit. Richard was furious and recovered quickly, but he was not so furious that he did not recognize the sound of death coming. He had, after all, been reared in the projects.

Click! Clack! It was the sound of a round being chambered into an automatic weapon.

"Hold on now, hold on, Margarita. All this is uncalled for!"

Richard had heard the rumors that Margarita Smith had once killed a woman and gotten away with it, but took the rumors as unproven gossip. Now as he saw the look in her eyes, he thought the rumors were quite possibly true. The woman looked deranged.

"You have exactly ten seconds to get out of my apartment."

Richard tried to reason. "You have to give me a chance to put on my clothes."

"One!"

"Come on, you can't be serious."

"Two!"

She was serious. Margarita stepped away from the door, giving Richard an opportunity to go. He shot through the door and into the hallway before she could count to three. Margarita stayed in the room counting loud enough for Richard to hear her from the living room. She could hear him moving furniture, scavenging for his things. Before she reached nine she heard the door open and slam shut. She walked into the living room and then to the apartment door. She looked through the peephole and saw Richard hurriedly getting dressed in the corridor. He looked over to her door every second or so to make sure she was not coming out.

‡‡‡

Margarita got out of the shower and tried to erase Richard from her mind. She was sure he would try to avoid her in the future. She looked at the clock on her dresser. It was already ten o'clock in the morning and she was due to pick Héro up at eleven o'clock. Margarita called down to the doorman to have her car brought to the building and then dressed quickly in a pair of tight jeans and a halter top. Héro made her promise they would go to Central Park. She threw a Calvin Klein jacket over her shoulder and took the elevator down to the lobby.

The doorman informed her that her car hadn't arrived and Margarita decided to wait out front for her Jag. The light breeze felt good on her face and she looked up into the sun, enjoying the mixture of warmth and wind. It made her think of the Caribbean.

A good-looking young Mexican man pulled up to the building in her Jaguar. She didn't recognize him as the regular attendant, but he seemed to know the car belonged to her. He held the door open as she came around to the driver's seat. Margarita handed him a ten-dollar bill and he flashed a big grin and closed her door.

His smile made Margarita think of Héro's smile whenever she received something new. Margarita stopped at a toy store before going uptown toward Harlem.

She needed a smile from her daughter to make her feel better after last night.

Margarita was never happy when she had to visit the brownstone that she bought, helped to renovate, and then gave to Chemah in the settlement of their divorce. She had given the building up for the benefit of her daughter, but still, every time she reached the building on Sugar Hill she felt an ache in the pit of her stomach.

Margarita pushed the doorbell. She almost wished that Tatsuya would answer the door. She had a sick need to win the child over again. The fact that he believed that she had killed his mother did not daunt her.

Then she was relieved when Michelle answered the door. Now she knew she wasn't really ready to face the little boy. She remembered how much like his father he was—quick-witted, intuitive, and unforgiving.

"I'm sorry, Héro isn't here, Margarita. She stayed over at Mrs. Richmond's house last night. Mrs. Richmond usually brings them back early in the morning, but they're probably watching cartoons or taking a walk."

Margarita looked at the blind woman and wondered how she knew it was her. Margarita had no animosity for her. Michelle and Chemah had gotten together well after their marriage was over.

"I'll call and tell Mrs. Richmond to bring them over. Do you want to come in?"

Margarita's last memory of being in the house alone with Michelle was not a good one. They both almost died.

"I'll just wait in the car. You don't have to pack anything. She has everything she needs at my house."

Michelle closed the door and Margarita headed back to her car. Five minutes later Margarita's phone rang. She looked at the caller ID. It was Chemah.

Sitting out here in front of the house was already fucking with Margarita. She wasn't in the mood for a conversation with Chemah right now. There were already too many bad memories here just looking at the house. It seemed that every time she looked at the house from this vantage point something bad happened to her. Margarita pressed the talk button and put the phone to her ear.

"Hello."

"What the fuck are you doing, Margarita? I don't have time for this shit now."

"What?"

"What do you want? A custody battle? Because if that's what you want you've already lost. You weren't supposed to pick Héro up until this morning. According to the child visitation agreement, you can't come by at just any time you want and pick her up. Mrs. Richmond should have known better than to let you have her last night. Telling her that I sent you for her was a fucked-up thing to do."

Margarita was stupefied. Her mouth hung open. She couldn't get a word out that would be coherent.

"You can have her until tomorrow because I have a lot of shit on my plate right now, but if you ever try pulling some shit like this again you will never—and I mean never—see Héro again, do you understand?"

Click.

Margarita listened to the dead silence for a second and then stared at the phone in her hand as she processed all of the things that Chemah had said. It didn't make any sense at first and then it became very clear. Someone who looked like her had picked Héro up from the babysitter last night. Her baby girl had been kidnapped and Chemah thought she did it.

Margarita got out of the car and frantically ran up to the door of the brownstone again. This time she didn't ring the doorbell. She banged on the door with her fist.

Bam! Bam! Bam!

"*Open the door. Michelle, open the door.*"

Michelle was on the other side of the door, but she wasn't about to open it. She had Chemah on the phone at that very moment. She was speaking to him in harsh whispers.

"Do you hear her? She's screaming like a crazy woman! You better get home and handle this! You damn right, I am not letting that crazy bitch in here! How the hell am I supposed to know if Héro is in the car? No! You call the goddamn police! This is Harlem. That bitch could break the door down and kill a dozen people up in this camp before they respond to a call from me! I got my razor in my hand right now! If she comes through the door today, you aren't going to have to worry about no more baby mama drama. I am not joking! Well, hurry then!"

Bam! Bam! Bam! Bam! Bam!

"*Michelle, open this fucking door right now! I know you can hear me!*"

Michelle had her back up against the front door and felt a pounding in the middle of her back every time Margarita pounded on the door. She had her razor in her hand like she had told Chemah. She always put up a tough front to keep people off her, but she never let herself forget the real truth. She was blind and the blade was all but useless in her hand. She pressed herself up harder against the door and prayed that the police came quickly.

Chapter 13

Bending Over Backward

Chemah looked through the two-way mirror at Margarita. She looked anxious and upset, but not nervous. The police officers from the Thirtieth Precinct had taken her away before Chemah could get to the house.

Mrs. Richmond stood next to him. She had been called down by the investigators who were looking into Héro's disappearance to identify Margarita as the last person to be seen with her. Chemah did not wait for uniformed officers to pick her up but instead he went back to Sugar Hill to pick her up himself. The detectives in charge were Johnson and Larnes, old friends of his who were detectives long before him. He had asked them as a favor, but they would not let him near Margarita. She had already asked for her lawyer and they didn't want to do anything that would ruin the case they were preparing against her by violating any of her rights. Chemah knew they were right. He couldn't believe that Margarita would do anything this stupid.

Mrs. Richmond identified her as the woman who had picked Héro up the night before. It hadn't been the first time the two women met. Mrs. Richmond was at both birthday parties that Margarita had thrown Héro in the past two years. Mrs. Richmond was loyal to Chemah as a close neighbor and friend, but Mrs. Richmond reminded Margarita of her own mother and was shown the utmost respect. The two women got along well enough.

Margarita would not answer any questions until her lawyer arrived and when he did, everyone who was on the other side of the mirror watching Margarita left the area.

It took Margarita's lawyer less than ten minutes before he came out of the room and asked to speak to the assistant district attorney and the detectives together in the interview room. Chemah was not allowed to come in. He was friends with both the ADA and the detectives who were handling the case, but he would have felt better if he were in there with them. Chemah waited in the detective area with Mrs. Richmond. She couldn't stop apologizing to Chemah for letting his daughter go. Chemah forgave her over and over again, knowing that the older woman never had anything but the best intentions toward his children.

Lena Delacruz, the ADA, came out to the detective area and Chemah stood up, waiting to hear some news.

"Hear me out before you say anything, Chemah."

That didn't sound like good news.

"We have two choices. We can keep her based on the babysitter identifying her. The judge will allow her testimony to stand at arraignment and Margarita will stand trial for kidnapping."

Chemah gave an impatient sigh and buried his hands deep in his pockets to keep from punching something.

"Now hear me out, Chemah. Margarita hasn't given us the whereabouts of your daughter yet. We have no idea where she left the girl. We don't know if the girl is in any kind of danger and what reason, if any, Margarita has for taking her in the first place. We won't know unless we let her go and let her lead us to your daughter. We've already sent a patrol car over to her apartment to see if the girl is there, and they've reported that her apartment is clean. If we arrest her now, and she's as crazy as you say, the chances are that you'll never see your daughter again."

Chemah nodded his head vigorously but had no words to say; the smart choice could only be to let her go. He wanted to kill Margarita now even more than he had the two previous times that he had tried. He was clinging to his own sanity by sheer force of will. If he lost control now, he knew that there would be no one in this precinct who would be able to stop him from seriously hurting or killing Margarita.

"She says she wants to speak to you before we let her go."

So the choice had already been made.

Lena Delacruz saw the emotional anguish in Chemah's face and it worried her. "Do you think that you can hold it together?"

Chemah dug his hands deeper into his pockets and started for the interview room door. The ADA turned to Mrs. Richmond.

"Mrs. Richmond, we're going to need another statement from you. If you could stay right here until we're finished, I would appreciate it."

Lena Delacruz hadn't wanted to say anything more to upset Chemah, but she and the detectives were all leaning toward believing Margarita now. She had no motive or reason unless she were truly crazy, and after speaking to Margarita for more than an hour, she knew that the woman was far from that.

"Yes, ma'am, I'll wait right here," Mrs. Richmond said through her tears. The guilt she felt at having given a child she loved away to danger was written all over her face.

Chemah entered the interview room and could see that the two detectives were standing awkwardly on either side of Margarita as if to shield her from some unseen threat. He knew they thought she needed protection from him and they were right. Chemah walked to the table where Margarita was seated and took his hands out of his pockets. The two detectives flinched, but didn't move from their posts on either side of Margarita.

"I want to talk to Chemah by myself."

Margarita's lawyer got up from his seat across from her.

"I don't think that would be the most prudent plan of action at this time, Margarita."

Margarita didn't even bother to look at him. She was staring intently at Chemah.

"I'll tell you what the fuck I think is prudent. You don't talk again until I tell you to. Now leave the room and wait for me outside. Otherwise leave and keep going, I'll find another lawyer."

Margarita's lawyer grabbed his belongings and nodded to the detectives.

"I'll be waiting outside, gentlemen." He acknowledged the two detectives.

Chemah looked to the two detectives for some sign that they were going to leave, but they gave none. Lena Delacruz, who was standing behind Chemah, gave them the nod and they started to move toward the door. Chemah didn't feel any way toward them for standing between him and Margarita. They were only doing their jobs. ADA Delacruz followed them out and Chemah waited for Margarita to speak.

"All they've told me so far is that Mrs. Richmond swears that I picked Héro up last night. I swear to you that I didn't. I know you better than anyone, Chemah, and I know that you have the ability to tell if I'm lying or not."

"I once thought I could tell, but we both know that wouldn't be true anymore, Margarita."

"What would I have to gain from taking Héro, Chemah? I love her as much you do, maybe more. What am I going to do, send myself a ransom note? I gave her to you to save her from being lost in the world. You think I would just put her in harm's way now? You know I would give anything to see her safe." Margarita knew that she could easily allay Chemah's suspicions by letting him know that she was "occupied" with Richard on that night. But she didn't want to disclose that information because she needed Chemah to believe that she didn't want another man.

"Why do you think Mrs. Richmond would accuse you of taking her?

She knows what you look like. She described your car down to the license plate."

"Why would an old lady remember my license plate. Did you ask her that?"

"Yeah, I already asked her. She noted the way that you peeled out. You know, the crazy way that you always drive and she thought that maybe she should remember it in case there were some sort of accident."

"That's convenient."

Chemah shrugged. "They're letting you go, Margarita, but I want you to know something. If they don't watch you, then know that I will be watching you wherever you go. You will not leave this city with my daughter."

"Then I have this to say to you, Chemah. Our daughter is out there somewhere without your or my protection and if you don't find her before something happens to her, then I will hold you personally responsible for having left her with an old lady who doesn't know the difference between Héro's mother and a fucking stranger. And so help me, Chemah, if something does happen to Héro, I will not rest until she is avenged and everyone responsible gets what they deserve. Including you."

Chemah felt the force of her words and believed her. Margarita rose and started toward the door.

"I have a lot of enemies, Chemah. You know that better than anyone else. But none of them have the courage or resources to make themselves look like me—none that I can think of right now anyway. I'm hiring a private detective to help track Héro down. My lawyer has probably called Senator Greenberg and Congressman Gianetti already. They owe me favors and will be persuading the FBI that this is a high-priority case and should receive their utmost attention. All of my resources have already been put into place to get our daughter back. The FBI will be at your house and mine waiting for a ransom call within the next two hours or so. I'm sure they're going to want to talk to Mrs. Richmond too, so don't let her get too far. "

In the most powerful political circles of New York, Margarita Smith was known as the "Comeback Kid." The notoriety she gained from her role in bringing closure to the high-profiled Street Sweeper case was the elixir necessary to sooth politicos' apprehensions about being associated with an ex-con. Although she sold her interest in her political consulting firm before she went to jail, Margarita's phone had been ringing non-stop with offers, making her one of the most sought-after political strategists on the East Coast. Margarita's attorney/accountant, a shrewd investor, took good care of her assets—which nearly tripled her net worth. As a result, Margarita chose to take on her private clients as she deemed appropriate and took great delight in turning down people whom she perceived had turned their backs during her darkest days.

Dressed in a St. John, blush mélange pearl-striped suit and a pair of pink Manolo Blahnik kidskin slingbacks, perfectly accessorized with ample Tiffany ice, Margarita struck a defiant pose as she turned the doorknob and opened the door. Her lawyer, the two detectives, and the ADA were all waiting right there.

Margarita spoke softly this time.

"I'm not counting on any of them, Chemah, I'm counting on you. Please find my baby. She's all I've got left."

Chemah saw the fear in Margarita's eyes and it scared him. At some level he'd thought that he would confront her or even threaten her and she would relent and give Héro back to him. Now he knew that was a false hope. He was a drowning man grasping at straws.

Chapter 14

Hope Against Hopeless

It was two weeks since Héro's disappearance. Chemah was going crazy trying to figure out the kidnapper's angle. The FBI left his home a week ago when no ransom note or phone call came. They would keep their investigation open and Chemah or Margarita should contact them immediately if either of them heard from the kidnapper. Chemah was doing an investigation of his own but was running into wall after wall. He tracked all the people who he knew made false license plates for stolen cars. Someone must have made a duplicate of Margarita's license plate and put it on a matching car. He also asked the FBI to track the names of notorious makeup artists who specialized in identity duplication for the city's crime families. The other obvious place to look was the special effects companies in the city.

How the hell did they get someone to look so much like Margarita that they fooled Mrs. Richmond? Chemah wondered. All the leads that he followed took him to dead ends. Margarita left him message after message asking if he had found anything out. He never had anything positive to relay to her.

Michelle stopped being a bitch when Chemah didn't come home for two days after Héro had gone missing. He called her only once, asking that she take care of Tatsuya. He was worried that Michelle would attempt to leave him at Mrs. Richmond's house when she had to go out and that was the last thing he wanted.

Today was the day that Michelle was to go in for the second part of the operation. Chemah had not gone with her to Doctor Johanson's office yesterday for her final consultation. Michelle went with Mrs. Richmond and Base while Tatsuya was at school. It was a hard trip because Base never liked Mrs. Richmond and Michelle had to keep paying special attention to him so that he didn't keep snapping at the matron whenever she got too close. Michelle wanted to be upset with Chemah but the stress of missing Héro was upon all of them. It would be selfish to think that he would stop his investigation into Héro's whereabouts for an afternoon at her doctor's office. She had made it clear to Chemah that she understood his position and he was relieved. He had already taken a lot of days off to make every other appointment before the first operation and was now using more of his vacation time to try to figure out what happened to his daughter. His official vacation was over five days earlier and he had to call his captain to extend it. Captain Brea already knew of the circumstances and readily allowed Chemah to stay out of the office.

Chemah could almost see Captain Brea smiling as he talked to him over the phone and told him to take all the time he wanted. *Son of a bitch.*

Now, as Chemah was carrying the bag that Michelle packed for the hospital down to the car, his cell phone rang. Chemah looked at the caller ID. It was the precinct. He called Black Rob to check on a lead for him and he was expecting a call back. It was too soon for Rob to have called back with any information, and it gave Chemah hope that he was finally on to something.

"Hello, Rob. Tell me that you have good news."

"Detective Rivers, it's Captain Brea. I need you to come down to the precinct right now."

Chemah didn't hesitate when he heard the captain's order.

"I'm sorry, sir. I have a full schedule today. My wife is having major surgery this morning. We're on our way to the hospital right now."

Captain Brea pulled the receiver away from his ear and looked at it, frustrated and puzzled. He'd read Chemah's file and knew, in great detail, about the unfortunate chain of occurrences surrounding Margarita's arrest and conviction. Edwin Brea would pull the file on occasion just to look at the pictures of Margarita. She was fine as hell. He certainly wouldn't mind being handcuffed by her, but if any fucking was to be done, he would be the one thrusting the dick, not her.

"I didn't want to mention this before, Detective, but I read your file. I know that you're no longer married—you don't have a wife. Now, I'm giving you a direct order to be in my office in one hour, or this time you will be charged with insubordination. Do I make myself clear?"

Chemah opened his mouth to explain himself, but didn't bother. He didn't want to make any more waves between him and the captain, so he relented. Anyway, he thought he could do the same thing he had done in Israel. He knew the operation was going to take six hours. He had not planned on spending the entire six hours in the hospital anyway. He had intended to follow up on more of the leads he had on special effects specialists.

"I'll be in as soon as I can, sir. Give me at least ninety minutes."

"You have ninety minutes, Detective." Captain Brea hung up without any further formalities.

"What an asshole!"

Chemah came back up the stairs to get Michelle who was taking her time coming downstairs and found her in the room putting on her shoes.

"Who was that calling you so early? Any news?"

"No, just work stuff. They want me to come in."

"Don't they know you're taking vacation time? They know you're still working on finding Héro yourself, don't they? Did you tell them that you are on your way to the hospital with me? I swear, they think you're the only detective in the whole fucking city!"

Chemah grabbed her around the waist and felt the tension in her back.

"It's going to be fine, baby. I handled it. Come on, let's get you to the hospital."

‡‡‡

An hour later Chemah was rushing from the operating prep room where he left Michelle with her doctor and the anesthesiologist. He promised that he would be waiting for her after post-op with her favorite Popeyes fried chicken meal.

Chemah knocked on Captain Brea's door and entered the small office before the captain could look up from the computer screen he was concentrating on. He stood in front of the captain's desk for a moment and waited for the captain to finish logging off the computer. He was wasting time, he thought. It had been seventy-two hours since Chemah had slept. He had gotten about four hours sleep when he fell asleep at his desk while looking through the files of all known kidnappers in the tri-state area. He wasn't planning on resting again until he got his daughter back.

The captain pressed one last key and then got up from his desk. He picked up a file that was on the edge of the desk and thrust it at Chemah.

"This is your new case."

Chemah was unmoved. He didn't reach for the file or even look down at it as the captain held it out in front of him.

"I told you I'm on vacation. I'm not coming back to work anytime soon."

Chemah glared at the captain. But the captain looked back at him passively.

"I know you're working on finding your missing little girl, Detective. I've got two little girls of my own. I'm not insensitive to what you must be going through."

"With all due respect, Captain, *fuck you!* You have no idea what I'm going through. I'm wasting time here. I've got work to do."

Chemah turned to leave, but the captain's words were seductive.

"I'll bet if you took a look at the file you'd change your mind, being as you're already on the case."

Chemah turned back to the captain and looked him in the eyes. There was no sign of humor in them. Chemah took the file that Captain Brea still had extended toward him and opened it. The pictures inside were startling. They mimicked the ones that he had seen in Israel and the ones that the FBI had taken from the murder on the plane. Chemah thought he hid his shock well, but the sight of the broken bones set to the pattern of the inverted cross on the bodies of the drug dealers was too much even for him to dismiss. Even so, he shrugged his shoulders and handed the file back to the captain.

"The pictures look like the ones that were sent to you by the FBI. You gave that case to Rodriguez and Flores."

"That's right, I did give them that case, but this one is different. The guy who did his wife on the plane is still in FBI custody, I checked. These three bodies are fresh. It looks like we might have a copycat or maybe it's a ritual killing. What's your guess?"

The captain was baiting him. He knew something that Chemah didn't know and Chemah couldn't figure out what it was. He needed sleep; it was telling on him.

Chemah shrugged. If not for Héro being missing he would have jumped on the case. He had all but forgotten the case that was assigned to Rodriguez and Flores. He knew it was somehow connected to the murders in Israel and Fallujah. In light of these new bodies in New York he would have to tell the captain what he knew.

"I saw the files that you sent to Forensic Specialist R. Johnson. They show the exact same wounds inflicted on the victims in these pictures. You sent those files from Israel over a month ago. You'd better tell me what the hell is going on here."

It was well rumored that the captain indiscriminately used his administrator's rights to access, read, and in some cases, intercept the e-mail and files of the detectives in his unit. Chemah was sure that Rob had not gone to the captain with any information before clearing it with Chemah first, which left only one reasonable conclusion.

"Don't you look at me with that sanctimonious bullshitting stare! The New York City Police Department owns every one of the computers used by its employees. We have a right to monitor any and all activity to determine what you're actually doing when you're supposed to be working. Now, you've been holding back information pertaining to an ongoing investigation. If it were up to me, you'd be put up on charges."

"But it isn't up to you, is it?" Chemah broke the rhythm of the captain's tirade. "You already talked to Agent Morris and he told you to put me on the investigation despite the information that you brought him about the case and the information that you intercepted from Rob's email folders."

Captain Brea looked over Chemah's shoulder through the window at the other detectives he managed. Chemah had not closed the door and was talking loudly. People were starting to look over their cubicles into his office.

"So I'm going to tell you now for the last time, and if I have to call Agent Morris myself, I will. *I will not be coming back to work until I find my daughter!* If you have a problem with that, then fuck you! Fuck Agent Morris! And fuck the whole goddamn department!"

When everyone in the bullpen heard Chemah cursing, they came out of their cubicles and started to congregate close to the captain's door. Most of them had never heard Chemah use profanity. He was always a consummate professional.

The captain was uncomfortable with all the attention they were getting. If Chemah quit now, he would have to explain it to his superiors.

"Alright, take it easy, Chemah. You and I may not get along that well, but you know the department is behind you one hundred percent on finding your daughter. All the resources we have are at your disposal. Agent Morris himself told me to have you call him if there is anything he can do. All we're asking is if there is anything that you know about this case that would help us solve it before the media gets wind that there is another crazy serial killer out there, we would really appreciate it."

Chemah looked over his shoulder at his colleagues and understood what was making the captain nervous. There would be a coup and no one would respect the captain if Chemah disrespected him now in front of everyone. As much as it sickened him, Chemah took the high road.

"If I can think of anything, sir, I'll call you. I'll tell Rob to explain everything we discussed with Rodriguez and Flores."

"Thank you, Detective. And good luck."

He extended his hand to Chemah. Chemah took it grudgingly. The captain knew how to put on an act. Everyone who was watching the show would think that they parted as friends.

Chemah walked out of the captain's office and headed toward Detectives Rodriguez' and Flores' desks.

"Rod, Flo,"

He clasped hands and gave man hugs to both detectives.

"Chemah, if there if anything we can do."

"Yeah, man, anything, you just let us know."

"I'll let you know. Listen, you got those new cases with the victims' bones broken in all of those odd angles. Talk to Rob, he has some information that might be helpful to you."

"Black Rob has something that's going to help us? What's he got, a new rap song that brings out the criminal in white people?"

The two detectives laughed and slapped each other's hands.

Chemah did not have the time or inclination to laugh.

"Check the files he's going to give you. If you haven't noticed he's been the forensic specialist on every big case I ever had. He knows his shit and if you listen past the ebonics, the man is a genius. Give him a chance and you might solve this case."

The two detectives looked at each other and sobered up. Neither one of them had ever had a case as big as the one they were now on nor had they any clues that determined which direction to go. Chemah was throwing them a bone.

"Thanks, Chemah. We'll go talk to him right away."

"Let me have a talk with him first. He's still helping me with my thing right now and somebody might block me if I don't get what I need from him quick." Chemah nodded toward the captain's office.

"We got you, Chemah. Just let us know when."

"Thanks."

Chemah thumped his fist against each of theirs and then turned to go to the forensic lab in the basement. As he passed the bulletin board that showed all of the open cases, he saw a picture that startled him. He took a closer look and then called over to the two men he had just left.

"Rod, Flo!"

The men heard the urgency in his voice and walked over quickly.

"What is this?" He pointed at the picture on the board that showed five dead men. It was obvious to Chemah that the men were laid out to shape an inverted cross.

"That's the One-Hundred-Thirty-Eighth-Street massacre," Rodriguez said, taking the picture down from the board to look at it more closely. "James and Gerwoski had the case when they thought that it was a hit by a rival drug gang. The way the victims were laid out, they thought it was Big Tony's boys that took them out, trying to send a message. Internal Affairs took over the case when someone identified that probey officer as the last one to be seen talking to these guys on the corner. They checked her gun through ballistics and found out it was the weapon used in the shooting. The media had a field day with it the night we interrogated that guy at the hospital. I watched it on the late news that night when I got home. I'm surprised you didn't hear about it."

That was the same night that Héro was taken. Chemah had not watched television or read a newspaper since. It suddenly dawned on Rodriguez what he had just said.

"Sorry, man, I didn't mean anything."

"Forget it."

Chemah took the picture from him and took a closer look at it. He couldn't quite make it out, but there was something wrong with the picture. Something was out of place. All of the victims were wearing black. The victim at the bottom of the picture was holding something colorful in his hand.

"One of you guys have a magnifying glass?"

"Sure, I have one at my desk."

All three men walked over to Flores' desk. Rodriguez and Chemah watched Flores rummage through the garbage in his top drawer for a few moments before announcing, "Here it is."

Chemah took the glass from him and inspected the picture. Both the detectives watching over Chemah's shoulder had no idea what he was looking for, but knew immediately when he found whatever it was. Chemah started to visibly shake. Both detectives took a tentative step back from Chemah.

"What is it, Chemah? What do you see?"

Chemah took a deep breath and exhaled. He had already given away too much. He felt as if he were losing control of himself with every second that he delayed sleep.

"I thought I saw something, but it was nothing."

Both detectives knew he was lying, but weren't about to press him.

"Who was the probey they're stringing up for this?"

"Girl named Frances Suarez. Fine chick. But those are the crazy ones, you know."

"Yeah, they have her in protective custody at the women's prison on Rikers Island. I wouldn't bet any money she's leaving there anytime soon."

Chemah put the picture down on Flores' desk and tried very hard not to give away his thoughts. He had to get down to Rikers Island to see Officer Suarez. There was no doubt in his mind that the barrette in the hand of the victim in the picture belonged to his daughter. There must have been thousands of them made, but this one was especially ugly and his little girl was the only one he had seen with it. It was her favorite. Although the picture was taken before his daughter was even declared missing, it was too much of a coincidence. He had to follow it up. Chemah still had to see Rob before he made the long trip out to Queens where Rikers Island complexes were located. He looked at his watch and tried to gauge how much time he would have to get there and back before Michelle came out of post-op.

"Alright, I'm out. Like I said, reach out to Rob tomorrow and see what he has for you."

Chemah left and headed for the basement. The two men stayed at the desk looking through the magnifying glass at the picture. They spent the afternoon discussing what Chemah might have seen in the photo that they didn't, but they never figured it out.

‡‡‡

Rob was looking through slides of blood samples when Chemah came through the lab door. He was so engrossed that he didn't hear Chemah come in. Chemah tapped him on the shoulder and Rob almost jumped out of his skin.

"What the fuck!"

Rob jumped back into a fighting stance and looked like he was prepared to get busy. Chemah had taught him to fight over the years that they had known each other and would have been proud of his response under ordinary circumstances. Two years earlier someone had snuck into the lab, beat Rob in the head, and made off with evidence that was pertinent to a high-profile case that he and Chemah were working on. Since then, Rob always felt a little uneasy when he was working alone.

"Yo! Don't sneak up on me like that, son. I know your shit is nice, but I'm on automatic now. You never know what could've happened, na'sayin'?" Rob threw a combination of punches in the air that looked impressive.

"Yeah."

Rob took a second look at Chemah and changed his attitude.

"Did you check everyone on that list I gave you?"

"I checked everyone on the list. They're all still in the feds or missing in action. Anybody else who could have done it is either working for the CIA or with Steven Spielberg."

"Rob, what do you know about that Suarez case?"

"The multiple murder thing?"

Chemah nodded.

"Not much, that was Lawrence's case. Far as I know everybody got two shots to the chest and they left them in the building for dead. Internal Affairs took the case over."

"Do you have access to Lawrence's files?"

"Does a pig love shit?"

The look on Chemah's face didn't change and that made Rob nervous. He could usually get a laugh out of Chemah, but not today. Rob walked over to his computer and started tapping away on the keyboard.

"Here we go, son. It's coming up."

Chemah walked up behind Rob just as the file was generated. The photo that Chemah saw on the bulletin board upstairs was the first thing that came into view.

"Aaaww shit, man! This is some ole bullshit!"

"This is the first time you saw this photograph, Rob?"

"Hell yeah! This is the first time I've seen this shit, man. You think I wouldn't tell you if I saw some shit like this? This ain't no motherfuckin' coincidence, man! It's right fuckin' there—plain as day. The cross—it's upside-down, man!"

Chemah had Rob scroll down and they saw the rest of the photos taken by the forensics team. There was something else that was odd in the photo now that he saw the pictures as the bodies were separated from one another. All of the men were in various stages of undress. *Maybe whoever killed them had told them to strip and then changed their mind before they were finished*, Chemah thought.

Chemah told Rob to scroll down further and they both read the report written by Forensic Specialist Lawrence in silence.

Victims all have what appears to be residual semen against their lower extremeties and undergarments. Wounds indicate that no struggle…

"Where's the rest of the report?"

"I told you. Internal Affairs took the case over. Lawrence must have stopped working on it. He didn't bother to conclude any of the findings that he prepared before they housed it from him. Shabby work, if you ask me. Brotha has no work ethic."

"Can you get into Internal Affairs files?"

"I could if it were really important, but it would probably take a minute to find it."

"How much is a minute?"

"Couple days, give or take."

Chemah frowned. "Never mind." He turned away from the computer and started to walk toward the door.

"You're going to see her, aren't you?"

Chemah turned back toward Rob, but didn't say anything.

"It's the logical thing to do, man. Nobody else knows about the upside-down cross but us. She's the one who put the bodies together. She's the one with all the answers."

Chemah turned to leave again.

"I'm going with you."

"No, you're not."

"You're going to need prints, a DNA sample, and if you couldn't tell from the pictures, a possible sample of what she has underneath her fingernails. If you're lucky she hasn't clipped them in the last few weeks." Rob grabbed his keys and followed Chemah out the door.

Chemah turned at the bottom of the stairs that led out of the basement and faced Rob, stopping him in his tracks. Rob spoke before Chemah had a chance to say anything.

"Yeah, I know you can do it, but we both know that I'm better. And for this shit you can't afford any mistakes. Na'mean?"

He put his hand out for Chemah to slap, but Chemah just looked at him.

"Anyway, you know I'm right."

Rob walked past Chemah and started up the stairs. Rob was more right than Chemah wanted him to know. Rob had figured out that the six bodies were found in a hallway in Harlem were somehow linked to the cases that he and Chemah discussed on the phone when Chemah was in Israel. He didn't know about the barrette. Rob was the best man he knew at getting physical evidence and Chemah couldn't afford anything less than the best at this point. Every moment that passed put him further away from finding Héro. If Suarez had even a particle of evidence on her that would lead him to finding his daughter, Rob would be the man who could find it.

In Rob's mind, he was sticking by a friend who had been there for him when shit had taken a wrong turn. He thought a case like this was the only thing that would take Chemah's mind off his missing baby girl. Chemah had him researching every lead that was possible for the past two weeks and nothing had turned up. In desperation they even scoured the path that led up to Mrs. Richmond's brownstone in search of any element that might be out of place, or some particle that might have been added. Rob really felt bad for his boy. He could see that this was killing him inside, but there was nothing else they could do. *If this other case took Chemah's mind off his baby girl for just a day, then it would be worth it.*

Chemah called up after Rob, who was taking the stairs two at a time.

"You stay out of the interview room until I call you in, understand?"

"I got you, son."

"And you follow my lead. You don't say or do anything until I tell you to, understand?"

"My word, son. You gettin' me all amped. Like we ain't never did the Batman and Robin thing before."

When they left the building, Rob followed Chemah to his car. He didn't say another word until they got two blocks from the precinct.

"Yo son, I gotta pee."

Chapter 15

You're Not My Knucka

Chemah was driving back from Rikers Island into the city, trying to beat the clock. He needed to get back to the hospital before Michelle woke up in post-op and was taken to her room. Chemah looked over at the passenger seat. Rob was asleep and snoring loudly over the engine's hum. He'd fallen asleep instantly when they got back in the car and headed to Manhattan.

Since Héro had been missing, Chemah asked Rob to do two dozen different favors for him that he didn't have time to do himself. Rob hadn't refused him once. Chemah knew Rob was doing these favors on top of the work that the department required of him. The result was that Rob was exhausted and drooling on Chemah's leather seats. Chemah couldn't complain.

If he dropped Rob off at the precinct downtown, he would never make it back to the hospital before Michelle woke from the anesthetic. Chemah's only choice was to take Rob with him and let him sleep in the car while he visited with Michelle.

As he drove over the Triborough Bridge, Chemah revisited the last few hours in his mind. Officer Suarez was willing to talk to him without the benefit of her lawyer. He must have asked her two hundred different questions in twenty different ways and she always answered them the same. She swore to Chemah that she didn't commit the crime she was accused of. After two and a half hours of questions his instincts told him that she was telling the truth. The trouble was that all of the evidence pointed to her. She confided to Chemah that Internal Affairs found DNA evidence on her uniform linking her to the crime. She felt she was being set up and Chemah couldn't say any different. He couldn't ask her anything about the barrette that he saw in the picture because she wouldn't admit that she had been at the scene of the crime to begin with.

Chemah almost didn't see the point in it, but he had Rob take her prints and every kind of sample that he could get off her body in case they came across another sample that matched.

Chemah wasn't any closer to finding Héro except that now he was convinced that whoever was committing these murders had a personal vendetta against him. Chemah was sure it was more than one person now and whoever they were, they had the resources to replicate anyone they wanted. They had already done it with Margarita to get to Héro, and had used Officer Suarez' identity to send him a message. All he had to figure out now was why him and how he was going to get Héro back from them.

Chemah paid the toll at the end of the bridge and proceeded off the exit to One Hundred Twenty-Fifth Street. He almost made a left turn onto Fifth Avenue when he remembered that he still had to get Michelle's Popeyes fried chicken dinner. It looked like he was going to be late already—if he showed up with the chicken he could always say that was what kept him from being on time. He knew she wouldn't be able to eat the food immediately after the operation anyway, but that's how Michelle was. She wanted things when she wanted them.

Chemah traveled west on One Hundred Twenty-Fifth Street until he reached St. Nicholas Avenue. He didn't see a parking spot and turned left onto St. Nicholas where he knew there were parking meters. Chemah pulled up to a meter and turned the car off. The lack of motion startled Rob awake.

Rob rubbed his eyes and yawned as if he had been awakened by his mom. He looked out the window of the car at an unfamiliar storefront.

"Where are we?"

"I have to make a quick stop and get Michelle some chicken."

"Cool, I could eat."

Chemah put his NYPD parking pass in the window and stepped out of the car. Rob got out of the car, closed the door, and straightened his pants before following Chemah toward the corner. Chemah turned to him.

"Wipe your chin."

Rob wiped the drool off his chin and turned the corner alongside Chemah.

In front of Popeyes there was a homeless man acting as the doorman for anyone who was entering and exiting the restaurant. He held his hand out whenever he opened the door for anyone and the restaurant customers randomly gave him change. The man didn't demand anything from anyone, but he said, "good evening" to everyone who passed him, "thank you and "God bless" to anyone who gave him change. Chemah gave the man a dollar as he held the door open for him and Rob.

"God bless you. Have a blessed evening."

Chemah and Rob got on the shortest of five lines that formed in front of the cash registers behind the bulletproof glass and looked up at the menus on the wall.

"What you havin', man?"

"I'm not hungry. I'm picking up food for Michelle."

"Man, we been out all day. I could eat a bucket of chicken beaks right about now."

Chemah didn't respond to Rob's comment. Rob shook his head, wondering if his friend would ever come out of the funk he was in.

"Ya gotta eat somethin', pardnah. Way we been rollin' you gon need to keep yo strength up."

Chemah turned back to look at Rob—for whatever reason Rob had now added a Southern accent to his ebonics. Chemah suspected Rob thought it would make him sound "blacker," if that were at all possible. Rob noticed the look.

"I'm jus sayin', knuck—"

Chemah noticed a couple of young bloods in the line next to them perk their ears to his conversation and his eyes widened, warning Rob that this was not the place for him to try experimenting with that word.

"Uuhh, bruh, you know, you jes need to keep yo strength up is all naskeanameany?"

"Naskeanameany, what the hell is this mother—"

Chemah saw the brothers in the next line give Rob the nod and Rob nodded back. They obviously knew and agreed with what Rob was saying even if Chemah didn't. It was their turn to order now and the smell of the chicken had actually started to make Chemah a little hungry.

"Maybe I will have something. You order first, let me see what else they have."

Chemah looked up at the menu again while Rob gave the girl at the register his order.

"Jou should not eat meat."

Chemah was startled. He hadn't heard or felt anyone coming up behind him.

More surprisingly, it was a woman's voice. Chemah turned to see a short, sturdy-looking, brown-skinned woman with her curly hair cropped short. The woman had a smile that lit the room, though she had a pronounced gap between her two front teeth. Chemah would guess her age to be about sixty.

"Pardon me?"

"No meat for jou. That's it, hokay. Pardon mine haccent. Jou understand me?"

The woman's smile was infectious, but she seemed to be very serious about what she was saying. Chemah had grown up in this neighborhood and he knew most of the crazies that lived in the area. It was like that here; Harlem always took care of its own. He guessed that mental illness was a rampant disease and there were consistently new cases in the area. This woman was obviously one of them.

Chemah didn't have time for it now. He politely returned the woman's smile and turned back toward the cash register. Rob had finished ordering. Chemah glanced at the menu again, and then spoke to the cashier, giving her the order that he always heard Michelle give when he brought her here.

"I'll have a three-piece meal with a biscuit."

"What sides, sir?"

"Uh, mashed potatoes and cole slaw."

The cashier rang up the order and waited for Chemah, who had looked up at the menu again as if he couldn't make up his mind what else he wanted.

"And I guess I'll also have a two-piece meal with a corn on the cob and the Cajun rice."

Chemah felt a poke in the ribs.

"Jou no leesin so good, no? I tell jou no meat for jou, but jou order the meat. *Avemaria que tonto!*"

If Chemah's Spanish was accurate and it probably wasn't, she had just said, "*Holy Mary, what an idiot!*" Or she was calling him a dunce? He couldn't quite remember.

Chemah didn't want to start arguing with this crazy person in a fast-food restaurant. He tried smiling at her again and then looked to Rob for help. Rob shrugged his shoulders and was now trying to be as inconspicuous as he could be.

"Yo, let the man order what he wants. There are people waiting to order, lady," a tall man who was standing two people behind the curly-haired woman said plainly. She turned and looked at him or maybe it was more like a stare. The man tried to stare back at her, but in a moment bowed his head and said something unintelligible under his breath. If there were a large rock near, the man would have tried to hide under it. When the curly-haired woman turned back to Chemah she was smiling again.

"Jou have not eaten in days. No? Jou have not been hungry. I know these things. That is jour body's way of cleansing itself. It knows even if jou do not, that it cannot see what it needs to see when jour body is not pure. When jou have the flesh of another living thing in jou, jou cannot feel the power of the ancestors in jou. I say jou eat some maiz, with a beecuit, and drink some water. *Agua, mucha agua.*" She shook her finger at Chemah.

The curly-haired woman folded her arms and waited. Everyone who was waiting behind her folded their arms too.

Chemah couldn't believe his luck. First, he was going to be late going to the hospital and now he had to deal with a crazy lady. All of a sudden he wasn't feeling the chicken anymore. He smiled at the crazy lady and then turned back to the cashier.

"Forget the two-piece chicken meal. Just add a couple of biscuits and a corn on the cob to that three-piece meal."

Chemah felt another jab in his ribs and turned to face the curly-haired lady again.

"She already cashed the two-piece meal. Jou pay for it, I will eat it."

It was unlike Chemah to argue with someone he knew was mentally ill, but the lady was beginning to annoy him.

"What happened to, 'your body can't see what it needs to see. Don't eat the flesh of a living thing. Oh, the power of the ancestors'?"

The curly-haired woman smiled up at him with the all the efficacy of a sage grandmother.

"It is jou who needs to see. Not me. Me, I am hambre." The woman patted the paunch that was her stomach.

"Yeah, that's what I thought."

He turned back to the cashier. His first thought was to pay for his food and Rob's, but then he turned and looked back at the curly-haired lady.

She looked clean enough, but she was probably homeless. He thought of how his own grandmother had become senile before she died.

"Put it all on one bill."

"Everything, sir?"

"His meal." He pointed at Rob. "The two-piece, the three-piece, some extra biscuits, and the corn on the cob."

"Would you like something to drink with that, sir?"

"No, thank you."

Chemah heard a throat clearing behind him. He didn't bother turning around.

"And two bottles of water."

Chemah gave the cashier the money and she gave him back change. He didn't bother to count it. Time was wasting.

The food came quickly. Chemah looked in the bag and searched for the smallest box of food. He turned and gave it to the curly-haired woman, who took it into her arms and bowed to Chemah.

"Gracias, mi hijo."

"You're welcome."

Chemah blushed at being called son after what he had thought of her. His embarrassment led to him rushing toward the restaurant exit without saying anything else to her. Before he reached the door he could hear the curly-haired woman demanding extra condiments from the cashier. He didn't feel Rob next to him and turned to see Rob pulling a mound of napkins from a dispenser on top of one of the tables.

Chemah let Rob catch up to him at the door of the restaurant. The homeless man at the door opened it for them to leave and smiled a grotesque smile filled with rotting teeth at Chemah. Chemah had not noticed it before, but the man now looked familiar to him. Chemah had seen him many times before when he and Michelle came to get food, but now there was something about his eyes.

Chemah looked back over his shoulder at the man again and stopped when the man opened his mouth and spoke.

"The truth of what I am, is the truth of what you are—whore's son."

Rob stepped in front of Chemah before Chemah could react.

"Yo, what the fuck did you just say?"

The man's grotesque smile widened and he moved away from the door he was holding and took a step toward Rob. Before Rob could make a move, Chemah pulled him by the arm and away from the man. He'd had enough of crazy people for one night and he had to get to the hospital to see Michelle.

"Let's get out of here, Rob, leave the man alone."

He dragged Rob along, and Rob let him. Chemah knew the man was following them, it was that kind of night. He looked to the sky to see if the moon was full. He and Rob had only taken five steps before the man spoke again.

"You can come to me now or you can come to me tomorrow. I have all the time in the world to fuck and kill your woman and child."

Chemah knew the man was mentally ill, but the words that he spoke raised the hair on the back of his neck. He stopped in his tracks and faced the man. He held the food in one hand and clutched Rob's shoulder with the other.

"Listen, mister, we don't want any trouble. Let us be on our way."

"Trouble? You believe I'm trouble, do you, Chemah?"

Although the man was giving them a wide berth, he was circling around them, cutting off their path to the car. Chemah wondered how the man knew his name and then he remembered that he had been to Popeyes many times when the man was at the door. He had probably heard Michelle call his name.

"I don't care how crazy this bum-ass motherfucker is, Chemah. If he keeps talking shit I'm gonna lace his ass!"

The man was ignoring Rob and talking directly to Chemah.

"I won't be any trouble to you, son of man. I'll tell you what you can do. Tell me that we are friends. Tell me that you accept me as part of you, that we are one."

"Yeah, brother, we're cool," Chemah said, trying to step around the man before having his path cut off again. "We boys, right?"

Chemah was trying to placate him, but his words seemed to infuriate the man. Chemah could see the anger in the man's face, but his words were still calm and soothing.

"No. Tell me that we are one. That I am a part of you."

Rob tried to break away from Chemah again.

"Yo, Chemah, let me take this bum out. He's talking like he's Sosa and we softer than chocha. He don't know me, man."

Chemah watched the man as he moved around them. He was not moving like a derelict. He was stalking them like a fighter or even a panther. Chemah held tight to Rob. He didn't want to be responsible for Rob getting hurt. He whispered to Rob to be still.

"Relax, Rob. Let's try to get out of this without hurting anyone."

Rob whispered back to Chemah, but he was obviously nervous and his voice sounded more threatening than calm.

"I'm tryin'a stay Ghandi, man, but look at dude. Ain't no way he gonna let us by."

Chemah looked around for ways out, but didn't see any. People were walking the streets going past them in both directions, but nobody saw anything unusual. Just another bum harassing someone on the street, they thought, glad that it wasn't them. Some were even giggling as they passed them. Chemah and Rob must have both looked like they were afraid of an old vagrant.

Chemah finally had enough. He didn't want to hurt the old man, but he had to get past him. The car was only twenty-five yards away.

"Don't hit him, Rob. Stay on my right and we'll walk right past him."

"Cool."

Chemah feinted like he was going left and then went right instead, trying to get a step ahead of the old man. The old man was faster than he appeared and recovered quickly enough to step right in front of Chemah before he could go by. Rob was still on the right of Chemah when Chemah collided with the man and tried to push past him. Instead of pushing by, he was met with a strength that belied the old man's stature, and it was Chemah who was pushed backward. Chemah knew crazy people were always unusually strong. He told himself that this abnormal strength was only another symptom of the man's mental imbalance.

Now Chemah was in front of the man, but Rob was behind him. It was obvious that it was only Chemah he was interested in harassing, as he all but ignored Rob. Rob stood behind the man, not knowing what to do. So he did nothing and waited for Chemah to make a move. Chemah was angry, but he still didn't want to have to hurt anyone.

"Mister, I told you, I don't want any problem with you. Just let me pass."

"'Just let me pass,'" the old man mocked him, tittering the same evil giggle as Chemah came forward again.

This time when the two collided Chemah didn't use force. Instead he gave way to the man's strength and rolled off the side of him, ending up a half step in front of the man before he realized that Chemah was leaving him behind. Chemah quickened his step as soon as he was in front of the man with the intention of breaking into a run if the man continued to come after him.

If Chemah had counted on the look of horror in Rob's eyes to signal him to duck, he would have been a fraction of a second too late to avoid a roundhouse punch to his head. Instead it was the thirty years of martial arts training and his uncanny sensitivity to his surroundings that made him feel the air that the fist generated as it sped toward him.

Chemah dropped to the ground as if a rug was pulled out from under his feet, barely missing being hit by the man's fist. He allowed his right leg to project outward and he swung it in an arc delivering a dragon sweep across the old man's lower leg. He knew the old man was addle-minded and still didn't want to hurt him by using any more force than what was needed to knock him down. Chemah turned in time to witness the old man flailing in the air before falling backward and banging his head on the hard concrete.

Chemah's first instinct was to go to the old man and help him to his feet. The way he hit the concrete, he would probably be concussed and would need a doctor. But before Chemah could even move toward him, the man had already popped back on his feet. He didn't seem fazed by the fall he had taken and if anything, he looked happy and deranged all at once as he leapt at Chemah. Chemah tried to move out of the way, but as fast as he was the old man seemed a little faster. He was able to grab Chemah's shirt as Chemah moved quickly toward the car again. Chemah attempted to tear away from the man's grasp, but the shirt and the man were both strong and neither gave way. Instead his action pulled the man closer to him.

Before Chemah could do anything else the man had his hands around his neck. When Chemah felt the strength in those hands he knew he had to incapacitate the man before the man got to squeezing his throat. Chemah felt the hands tighten around his trachea and brought his own fist upward and out. He felt the cartilage of the man's nose give way against his third knuckle, but was surprised when the man's hands did not fall away from his neck. Instead they tightened. The tittering laugh that came out of the old man earlier became a sickening mewling sound as air was no longer allowed to pass through his nose to vibrate across his vocal cords. Chemah was able to take one last breath before he felt the old man's grip permanently cut him off from any source of oxygen.

Chemah began to pummel the man in the ribs, firing left hooks and three right hooks with his fists in rapid succession. Even through the blood pounding in his ears, Chemah was sure he heard the cracking of ribs as they tore free from the man's rib cage with each punch that he threw. Chemah felt the blood rush to his eyes and knew he would be unconscious in a few seconds.

Out of the corner of his right eye Chemah caught sight of the blur that was Rob's fist. It passed six inches away from Chemah's face and caught the old man squarely in the mouth. The few teeth that the man had left in his mouth flew away from his face. His mouth was a cavernous bloody mess. His grin now consisted of a single tooth dangling from his lower gum and a set of torn lips.

Chemah was about to succumb to the hands around his throat when the old man loosened one of them to backhand Rob across the face. Rob careened off the fender of the car parked at the curb and crumbled onto his knees.

Chemah's knees started to buckle. He reached out to grab the neck of the man, but his fingers felt thick and clumsy.

"Aaaaaaaaaaaaaarrrrrrrgghhhhhh!!!!"

It sounded like the scream that would have come from Chemah's mouth were he able to draw enough breath to produce one.

Chemah felt the pressure release from his neck and he crumbled to the ground. He gasped two lungfuls of air into himself and struggled to his feet, ready to fight for his life again. He looked both ways up the street and saw the old man running extremely fast down St. Nicholas Avenue. The few people who were on the street got out of the way when they saw him coming, knowing trouble when they saw it.

Seeing the man already too far away to chase, Chemah took another couple of deep breaths and rubbed his neck. He saw that Rob was already on his feet. He had a bruise on his cheek, but otherwise looked alright.

"Don't worry. Jou going to see him again."

Chemah almost jumped out of his skin. It was the second time the curly-haired Spanish lady had gotten behind him without him having noticing her.

"The cashier would only give me five packets of salt. It is not enough to make him go away forever."

"Salt?" Chemah noticed the empty salt packets she held in her hand.

"It is the only thing that can cause him any real pain. He hates it. I think I can juse it to capture him. He cannot die, jou know," the woman said matter-of-factly.

Chemah didn't want to deal with crazy people anymore, but the woman seemed a pleasant change from the guy who'd just tried to kill him.

"Are you telling me that you got that guy off of me with a pack of salt?"

"Five packets of salt, *hijo*. One packet would only have made him very angry. Five, he cannot get out of the body that he is in for a short time and he will run until the pain stops."

Chemah felt sorry for the lady. She was obviously deranged. She thought she had somehow stopped the guy from killing him with five packs of salt. Chemah knew that it was the six body shots he had hit the man with that had finally taken effect. With mentally ill people sometimes the synaptic pathways were so convoluted with other messages that the brain was sending that pain sometimes took a long time to register. Other times it didn't register at all.

Chemah looked warmly at the older woman and she smiled back at him. He knew that explaining why the man had not responded to his punches initially would mean nothing to her in her mental state. Still, he didn't want to be unkind to her. He thought he would humor her.

"Well, I don't know how you did it, but thank you."

Chemah reached into his pocket and pulled out a twenty-dollar bill. "Here, *tia,* take this."

The woman blushed at being called aunt and begged off the money.

"No, I cannot take jour money for what I have done. I am a *santera*, it is my job to do this for jou. The most I can take as payment is a chicken and jou have already given me that." She held out the box of fried chicken that Chemah had purchased for her and smiled. "It is not a live chicken, but still it is a chicken."

Chemah remembered the store on the corner of One Hundred Sixteenth Street in Spanish Harlem where his childhood friend, Tony, had lived. It had statues of all the saints and other weird religious icons in the storefront window. It always smelled of incense when the store door was open. The sign over the store had read "*Botanica*." Chemah remembered that once when he and Tony had passed the store a beautiful woman who stood out in front of it had called over to him. She had looked into his eyes and said something in Spanish or some other language that Chemah did not understand. She looked sad for a moment and then had grabbed his face and kissed him on the forehead. When she let him go he and Tony had giggled a lot and ran down the street back to Tony's apartment building. Tony had called the woman a "*santera.*"

"Anyway, the job is not finished. He will come after jou again. He wants what jou have inside. He wants the light. He will come after me too, but I have been looking for him for some time now. I will be ready for him."

The old woman was talking crazy again and Chemah thought it was time for him to go before she became more agitated.

Chemah saw that Rob was waiting to the side. Clearly Rob had had enough of Harlem's crazies for one day. After hearing what the lady was saying, Rob saw her no differently than the man that he and Chemah had just fought. He was trying to signal to Chemah so they could leave.

"I'd love to stay and talk to you more, *Tia,* but my friend wants to leave."

The curly-haired lady looked over at Rob and he turned away. Her face did not lose its smile even when Rob shunned her.

"Jou are a good friend, *hijo*. Go and remember what has happened here today. No meat and plenty of aqua."

Chemah shook his head. The crazy lady was relentless.

"It is nice that jou call me '*tia*,' but maybe when we meet next, jou can call me by my name."

"Okay." Chemah waited for the woman to say her name.

"Lydia. My name is Lydia Anglero."

Chemah extended a hand to the woman.

"And my name is—"

"Chemah. Of course, I know jou, Chemah. Jou are in the newspaper all the time."

For a brief instant Chemah panicked. He thought maybe every crazy person in the city knew his name. The old lady took his hand in hers, brought it to her face, and pressed her lips to it. She let his hand go and said, "*Namaste*."

Chemah looked puzzled. He thought he knew that word, but could not place its meaning with his limited Spanish.

"'*Namaste*'? My Spanish is very bad, *Tia*. What does it mean?"

"*Namaste* is not a Spanish word. It is from the Swahili language. It means 'the divinity in me, sees the divinity in jou.'"

Chemah liked the way that sounded.

"Thank you, *Tia*." Chemah started walking to the car. He was so taken by what she had said that after taking only five steps he decided to turn and wave good-bye to her. He turned too late. She was already gone, nowhere in sight. Still, thinking of her made him keep a smile the rest of the way to the car.

At the same time, somewhere else, Lydia Anglero was thinking about Chemah too. She wondered if he would ever remember where he had first heard the word *namaste*. She wondered if he would remember the beautiful young woman who had spoken the word before blessing him with a kiss on the forehead. Lydia Anglero hoped the blessing had done him some good. The one she had left him with today would not protect him as long as that first one she had bestowed upon him.

Chapter 16

Loose Ends

Chemah was late getting to the hospital. Michelle was too groggy to lash into him, but she had managed to stay awake waiting for him. He walked into the room in time to hear her tell the nurse a joke.

"There was this male patient in bed in the hospital wearing an oxygen mask over his mouth and nose. A young student nurse shows up to give him a partial sponge bath. 'Nurse,' he mumbles from behind the oxygen mask. 'Are my testicles black?' Embarrassed, the young nurse replies, 'I don't know, sir. I'm only here to wash your upper body and feet.' So anyway, the guy looks disturbed and he struggles to ask again, 'Nurse, are my testicles black?' Concerned that he may elevate his blood pressure and heart rate from worry about his testicles, the young nurse overcomes her embarrassment and pulls back the covers. She raises his gown, takes his dick in one hand and his balls in the other. She takes a close look and says, 'There's nothing wrong with them, sir.' The guy takes off the oxygen mask and smiles at the nurse. Then he says very slowly, 'Thank you very much, that was wonderful, but listen to me very carefully. Are my test results back?'"

The nurse snorted at the joke, trying to keep her laughter in. She noticed Chemah coming into the room.

"Your husband is here."

Michelle sniffed the air deeply.

"I can smell that fried chicken."

Chemah shook the bag in the air causing it to make a rustling noise.

"Mmmm, mmmm. I love you, baby, now let me get at that chicken."

"I don't think so, missy." The Philippine nurse spoke English with a Brooklyn accent. She snatched the bag of chicken from Chemah's hand.

"No food until the anesthesia wears off."

"Dang!"

Chemah walked over to the bed and kissed Michelle softly on the mouth.

"How are you feeling, baby?"

"Chem, I don't know what this stuff is that they gave me, but we've got to see if it comes in a six-pack. I am higher than giraffe pussy right now."

Chemah looked over to the nurse who was checking the monitor and she gave him a look that said she sympathized with him. She believed it was only the anesthesia talking. She had not been there earlier, before Michelle was given any drugs, otherwise she would have known that this was Michelle at her best.

When the doctor came through the door Michelle was still trying to cajole a piece of chicken from the nurse.

"The operation went very well. I believe we'll know in a few days if your vision comes back partially or entirely."

"I'll be able to see in a few days?"

"I think so, Michelle. That is, barring some other complication."

"Some other complication?"

"No need to worry. If anything were amiss I would tell you immediately. Right now we're ninety-nine percent sure that the grafts that Dr. Yasmin put in have taken. All we had to do was take off the scar tissue that built up around the retina from previous operations."

The drugs that the nurse put into Michelle's IV were already taking effect and she started to nod before the doctor finished his last sentence.

Chemah stood up and shook his hand.

"Thank you, Doctor."

"She'll be alright. I'll come by and check on her again in a few hours."

Chemah stayed in the room with Michelle until she started snoring. Before he left he whispered in her ear, "I'll see you in the morning."

Michelle stopped snoring and almost came fully awake. She looked at him ruefully, but then drifted off again. Chemah could see that the worry lines that her face showed when she was awake smoothed to nothing while she slept. He kissed her lips softly and watched as a lazy smile came to her face. If he were not still thinking of his missing baby girl, the moment would have been perfect.

Rob was napping in the car again when Chemah got back. He was startled awake when Chemah opened the car door.

"Holy shit! You scared the crap out of me! I was dreaming that we were fighting that bum again."

Rob rubbed the side of his face where the swelling had doubled.

Chemah got behind the steering wheel and turned the ignition.

"Are you going to be alright, Rob?"

"It ain't nothing, son. Small thing to a giant." He touched his face again and winced. "Yo, we did work on that bum, didn't we? Did you see the way he ran? He didn't want any more of this. Bake it how you want, ain't no cupcake in me. You ain't gonna run up on my man and think I'm gonna just watch, na'sayin?"

Chemah took off and headed back downtown to the precinct where Rob had left his car. Rob continued to recount to himself and Chemah how the fight against the homeless man had gone. He bigged himself up more each time he retold the story. Chemah was sure that Rob soon would be telling the story of how he had fought alongside Chemah against the biggest dude in Harlem that anyone could imagine. Already the homeless man was over six-foot-three and weighed between 230 and 250 pounds as Rob was telling it. Chemah would have guessed the old man was more like five-foot-ten or five-foot-eleven and weighed about 165 pounds. As Chemah thought more about the old man's physical makeup, he started to wonder if the old man was high on PCP. PCP, or Angel Dust, as it was known on the street, had the uncanny ability of giving the people who took it what sometimes appeared to be superhuman strength.

"I don't think we ever gonna see dude again, son, unless you go looking for him in a hospital or something, because he's gotta be hurt."

Chemah guessed Rob was right. Any other time he might have gone looking for the homeless man, but there was no time to help anyone else right now. This was all Héro's time he was wasting.

Chemah stopped the car in front of the precinct and let Rob out. They made plans to catch up again tomorrow and then Rob reached into the car window to give Chemah a last handshake with three different grips. When he pulled his hand out of the window he held up two fingers in the peace sign and said, "Peace, grease and drawers, baby, I'm out."

Chemah knew Rob wouldn't go home right away. He would go inside the precinct and recount the night's episode to anyone who asked him about the welt on his cheek. By now the story was so different in his head that Rob saw himself as a hero. Chemah didn't mind. Rob was due some respect anyway. He was as good a friend as anyone else had ever been to him.

Chemah drove toward home thinking of a proverb that his teacher, Grandmaster Sam McGee, was fond of quoting. Until lions have their own historian, tales of the hunt will always glorify the hunter.

Chapter 17

Dreamers are the Saviors of the World

Tatsuya was staring at the ceiling over his bed. Listening to the cars pass outside his window, he welcomed the cottony feeling in his head and began his downward drift into the night's dream.

Tatsuya touched down in what he sensed was somewhere familiar. Perhaps he was around the corner in the neighborhood where his dad took him to get haircuts, but he wasn't sure. Dark clouds covered the moon and the night was blackened. Tatsuya felt anxious and guarded. He sensed it was well past his curfew but the streetlights weren't on. Base pulled him as they walked. He pulled back on Base's leash with all his strength, but the dog only became more determined to move forward. After three unsuccessful attempts to control Base, Tatsuya reluctantly allowed the dog to continue pulling him toward the large building at the end of the block.

As they approached the building, Tatsuya stopped abruptly. The people who went into and the skeletons that came out of the building frightened him. They were so focused on the building and in a hurry to get inside or leave, they didn't notice Tatsuya or Base standing there. Tatsuya sensed someone behind him. A hand rested gingerly on his shoulder. Before he could react, he heard a firm but soothing voice. The immediate darkness around the boy slowly gave way to flickers of candlelight.

"Namaste Tatsuya. Do not be afraid. There is nothing here that will harm jou. I have brought jou here to see jour sister."

"You know where my sister is?" Tatsuya asked.

"Yes, but jou must allow me to guide jou."

Tatsuya and Base were guided into the building. They waded through huge puddles of blood as they entered the hallway and began walking up the stairs. The presence pushed and Base pulled Tatsuya through the door of the apartment and guided him to the right. At the end the hallway, he saw Héro. She was sitting on a bed playing with an old brown doll with glasses and curly brown hair. Tatsuya smiled as he thought it funny that Héro's doll had on glasses. There was an hourglass on the bedside table next to the little girl. The sand was moving through the funnel quickly with two-thirds of the contents in the bottom portion of the timepiece. Héro was safe for now, but Tatsuya felt tears well up in his eyes because his little sister, though surrounded by people, was alone, playing in the dark.

In the distance, Tatsuya heard what sounded like huge old fans. The sound became louder. There were no skeletons in the apartment, but the people there began running around because they were all frightened. Tatsuya called to his sister, but it was impossible for her to hear him above the high-pitched scream of wind and thunderous clapping sounds. Suddenly afraid of what felt like an oncoming Lexington Avenue express train on rickety tracks, Tatsuya closed his eyes. When he opened them, he was back outside at the beginning of the block where he started his journey.

"Héro!" Tatsuya yelled.

"*No te preocupas, hijo*. We will rescue jour sister."

"When? How? Who are you?" Tatsuya questioned.

"Jou will know me upon sight."

"Namaste."

Tatsuya's lips moved in the darkness of his room. Had anyone been watching the boy, they would have been able to read his lips as he mouthed, "Namaste."

Lydia was nearly prepared for the ensuing battle with Bereft. While she was certain Chemah could eventually find his daughter, his timing worried her. She knew Chemah was distracted in spirit by life's events. Tatsuya, however, was stronger and purer in spirit. His mind was clearer and focus sharper. The boy was Héro's only hope. Lydia pinched out the flame on the fifth knob of her white candle. She whispered prayers of strength and courage for Chemah and Tatsuya.

‡‡‡

It was hard for Tatsuya to express the anger he felt toward himself for allowing his sister to be abducted. He hardly ever let her out of his sight whenever their father was not around. He had promised her upon first laying eyes on her that he would always protect her and never leave her alone. Tatsuya was quite pensive for his age. Last year, his grandfather, his last living link to his dead mother, had also died. He hadn't known his grandfather well, but he still loved him.

Tatsuya saw Héro's mother come up the walkway through the window in Mrs. Richmond's living room on that night and had gone upstairs to avoid having to be in her space.

When his father explained to him that it wasn't Héro's mother he saw after all, but someone who had been made up to look like her, Tatsuya believed him immediately. He'd watched Héro and Margarita leave the house from the window of the upstairs room where he stayed when Mrs. Richmond sat for them and noticed that Margarita never touched Héro. She'd led Héro to the car, opened the door, but never touched her. That was so unlike Margarita, who was always very affectionate with Héro. He remembered how affectionate she had been with him when she was his stepmother. She was always kissing, hugging, touching, and tickling him. After momentarily reliving those moments, Tatsuya was angry at himself for coveting the affection of the woman who'd killed his mother.

Tatsuya looked at the clock on the bedroom wall. It was eleven o'clock.

He heard his father downstairs talking to Mrs. Richmond and he jumped off the bed and put on his sneakers. His father didn't like the idea of him staying with Mrs. Richmond by himself. He knew his father was scared that he would be taken too.

Tatsuya came tiptoeing down the stairs and at the last moment before his father saw him, he jumped, trying to land on Chemah's back. Chemah turned and caught him in mid-air. It was a game they had played since Tatsuya had first met his father five years ago. He always tried to catch Chemah by surprise, and had not succeeded once in all that time. Occasionally his father tried to sneak up on him and was almost always successful. Only on a rare occasion could he sense another presence entering into his space, and he always knew that it was his father. His father praised him on those occasions, saying that he was not able to do the same thing at the same age.

"You have the gift," his father would say, acknowledging that there was something special about them both that he had not seen in others.

"Hey, you almost got me that time."

Chemah held Tatsuya in his arms, glad to have the boy safe with him again.

"How is Michelle doing? Can she see now?"

Chemah was never surprised by Tatsuya's concern for other people. The boy had a great concern for the people he loved and was always trying to help others.

"We won't know for a couple of days."

The boy smiled and climbed down from his father's arms.

"I dreamt about it last night."

"You dreamt about what?"

"About Michelle and about Héro too. I dreamt Michelle could see again, but she had to leave us and go far away."

Chemah looked at the boy closely and smiled. He knew Tatsuya had anxiety issues about being left alone since his mother died. It didn't help that Margarita, the one other person he had trusted and gotten very close to, had been convicted of manslaughter in the case.

"I wouldn't worry so much about Michelle leaving, Tat. You know she loves you and me and Héro, don't you?"

Tatsuya nodded.

Chemah wondered about his son. He had always been a serious little boy in comparison to others his age, but in the last two years Tatsuya had developed into a gracious and intuitive young man. He was a leader among the young boys that he played with in the community. He was respected without being feared, which was an oddity for boys in any neighborhood in Harlem. Chemah noticed it every time he saw Tatsuya and his little motley crew of about eight or so neighborhood ten-year-olds, but still, Tatsuya was the obvious leader.

"What about Héro?"

Chemah looked fast at Tatsuya at the mention of her name.

"I dreamt about Héro too."

Chemah didn't want to ask, but knew that sometimes he himself dreamt about things that were buried in his subconscious and he couldn't remember until after he dreamt about them again. Maybe Tatsuya had some information that he had forgotten to tell Chemah and now the information was coming out in a dream.

"What did you dream, son?"

"I dreamt that I knew where Héro is."

Chemah tried hard not to frown. He knew his son had no information that specific concerning Héro's whereabouts.

Tatsuya noticed his father's grim countenance. He didn't really remember the exact place that he'd dreamt about and now he was sorry that he had even mentioned it. His father was waiting for him to speak.

"I dreamt that she was in another building like the one we live in.

There were a lot of people and skeletons coming in and out. I think they were the drug people that you always tell me to avoid."

Chemah listened to his son. He didn't want Tatsuya to think he discounted anything in his life.

"I could see Héro in a dark room playing with an old doll. She wasn't afraid. The people that took care of the house were afraid to let anything happen to her. A man came in that nobody knew, but everyone was afraid of him."

Chemah waited. His son seemed to be thinking of something else.

"Was that all, Tatsuya?"

"Yeah, I guess so."

Chemah couldn't imagine where the boy's imagination had gone to conjure the dream, but he was glad that Tatsuya saw Héro was well. He didn't want his son imagining that Héro was somewhere suffering. If only he could piece together the clue that was left in the picture of those six men in the One-Hundred-Thirty-Eighth-Street massacre. That barrette in the photo was not a coincidence by any stretch of the imagination.

"Go get your stuff, son. We can both do with a little sleep. Tomorrow I have to pick Michelle up from the hospital and I'll have to take you with me."

Tatsuya's knapsack was on the couch. He flung the straps over both shoulders and walked back to the door that his father was holding open. He turned back around to Mrs. Richmond, who was standing by the bookcase near the door. He reached up and gave her a hug and a kiss on the cheek.

"Don't worry, Mrs. Richmond. Héro will be back home soon."

Silent tears rolled down Mrs. Richmond's face. "I know, baby, I know."

She wrung her hands together and looked at Chemah. He looked away, unable to reassure her of Tatsuya's prediction.

Chapter 18

False Hope

Margarita got off the phone with Chemah for the second time this Saturday morning. He was in his car, on his way home from the hospital with Michelle and Tatsuya.

Margarita's best friend, Kat, was over her house, and they were reviewing the paperwork that Margarita's lawyer sent over for her to sign. If and when Héro got back home, Margarita was determined to get custody of her. She wanted her baby home with her all the time. Now her lawyer had put together a case that was sure to sway any judge in favor of giving her full custody of her daughter. This was the perfect opportunity to show that she was more fit to raise Héro than Chemah. When she got Héro back home she would never let her out of her sight again. It was Chemah's fault that she was missing now and she would never forgive him.

"This thing says that Chemah isn't fit to raise Héro. You know that's not right."

"What's right or wrong isn't important anymore, is it? If I hadn't gone to jail, I would never have given her up. You know that."

"Margarita, I was the one who talked him into coming to see you and the baby at the hospital five years ago, on the day that he decided to take the paternity test, remember that? You tried to kill him. There was a possibility that you killed his son's mother—"

"That was an accident."

"—and he still did the right thing by Héro. He went against everything he thought was right, sweetheart. Just for that little girl. Taking her away like this is going to break his heart. If he hated you then, he's going to think you're a monster now."

Kat walked around the living room and picked up a picture of little Héro in her mother's arms. Margarita had it on top of the sideboard next to a vase of wild orchids. The photo was set in a filigreed silver frame that looked like it cost a fortune.

"He's only going to have one choice. We can all be a family again, or Héro's coming to live with me."

Kat put the frame down and spoke to her friend in a way most people who knew Margarita would not dare.

"Bitch, are you crazy? Even if that man doesn't kill you right off, he's not going to just let you take her."

"And what do you think he'll do? Kill his daughter's mother? End up in prison himself, where neither of his children will have parents? I don't think so. He'll get used to the idea. Then he'll come around."

Margarita looked in the mirror over the mantel and moved a lock of hair that fell over her brow.

"I'm still an attractive woman. I'm definitely prettier than what's her name, who can't even see what she looks like."

Kat couldn't believe what she was hearing. She always had Margarita's back, but this wasn't right.

"I've seen you do some stupid things and I've seen you do some crazy things. Shit, when it comes to being a mean bitch, I don't know anyone who does it better. But that blind girl has never done anything to you."

"So what? She has my man and my children."

"Your man? Chemah is not your man! You can't believe that he could ever want you again."

The air was palpable around Margarita. Kat could feel her ire from where she stood, but she did not budge an inch.

"You're fifty pounds overweight since your baby and now you're hating so much that you can't bear to see me and Chemah together again. Your man doesn't want you anymore and you don't want anyone else to be happy," Margarita said scornfully.

As her best friend, Kat had shared her marital woes with Margarita a few weeks ago. She certainly didn't expect the information to get thrown back in her face, but she knew that Margarita had no limitations when it came to getting even. Still, she was Margarita's friend and even though she was being a real *bitch* right now, later they would apologize to each other and agree that Margarita had gone too far.

Kat swallowed the huge lump in her throat and stood in front of Margarita.

"I'm going to let that slide, because I know you're *desperate* right now. I am still your friend and I will not let you destroy your life again."

The two women stood nose to nose sharing each other's breath. Margarita was the first one to turn away.

"If you aren't going to help me, you can leave right now."

"Oh, I'm going to help you. I'm going to go to Chemah right now and ask him if there is anything that I can do to help him find Héro."

Margarita picked up the paperwork again and pretended to be reading over it.

Chapter 19

Body for a Body

When the eighteen-year-old boy came to the building doors yesterday, only a half-hearted attempt was made to stop him from entering. The two men who guarded the door were told to expect that someone young and buff would come to the building today. The brother who came to the door fit that description and although he didn't bother to identify himself, it was enough for them. Their boss had been afraid when he gave his orders, and that in itself gave them pause.

"Young dude is going to come in today. He's going to be in shape—probably tall. Don't stop him from coming in. Don't touch him." Their boss had been adamant that the boy not be touched.

When the young man reached the door he only stopped long enough to wait for the door to be opened for him. Jimbo, the bigger of the two men at the door, almost stopped the good-looking young brother from entering and was reminded by a look from his partner of what their boss said. When the young man passed the two guards did not speak, but shared a look that communicated that they both understood their boss's fear. Some dudes simply had a look that said, "I'm not to be fucked with." Their boss had that look, but this young blood had the look a hundred times more than him.

Bereft spent the night at the Sangre Grande building torturing four young women with the body of the young man he had taken in the subway station yesterday. They welcomed his hard body, as they were used to dealing with older men who could do no better than the used shell of a woman that each had become.

The morning came and none of the women were dead. Bereft derived little pleasure from breaking these humans who were already so broken. Aside from the splintered bones and torn flesh that each woman had been afflicted with the night before, each woman bore a scarred soul for the rest of their lives. The pity of it was that Bereft could not know that he'd left an indelible mark on the women whom he "played" with on that night. Each wore their scars differently and with varied intensity. The four women would leave Sangre Grande and never return to the life that they previously led. Two of the women turned to the church. One of the women begged her family to take her back and she returned to school to finish her degree. The fourth woman walked straight out of Sangre Grande to the tallest building in Harlem and jumped off the roof without giving it a second thought.

Bereft sat in a hard-backed chair in the corner of the dark room closest to the door and watched Héro sleep. The scowl on his face told of his impatience and hunger. The girl herself was no special prize. He could and had snatched thousands of children in the time that he walked the earth. He could not touch them while they were still innocents, but part of the fun was to actually take their innocence from them. He had neither the time nor the inclination to bring the little girl to the impurity of which all humans were so easily capable. The girl was only an incentive to dangle in front of her father. Bereft stared at Héro reviewing his strategy over and over again. It was a risk to say which would bring Chemah to him faster—a damaged child or the threat of a damaged child. Today he would test what effect a threat to the child's well-being would have before leaving her to the devices of the weak men who frequented the building. It would be his final ploy, wagering that Chemah would give anything, including his soul, to find the person who had harmed his child. Bereft was loath to chance Chemah's reaction to that final gambit, but he saw no other direction.

Fifteen days ago when he took the body of Richard Fenton outside Margarita's building, Bereft read the recent memories of the man. A lesser being might have thought it luck that Bereft happened upon someone who was separated from Chemah by only one degree, but anyone who thought about luck in that manner had not been on the earth as long as Bereft. He knew that there was no such thing as luck. The lives of men and spirits alike were entwined by nothing more than what the simplest beings called karma—people and events were drawn to each other via acts, beliefs, and energy. The man whom he possessed was a necessary link in the chain that would bring him Chemah's energy and that was the only reason that it had fallen into his possession. It was an arrogant thought, but nonetheless accurate.

The plan that he devised came to him easily on that night. Moments after taking Richard's body he had gone back up to Margarita's apartment. When she opened the door to attack him, Bereft had easily overwhelmed her and took possession of her body. The rest of the plan had come easily once he had her memories. As he had anticipated, Margarita had easy access to Chemah's children. The male child would be far more difficult to engage so Bereft took the easier of the two targets and left her at this building that he deemed was safe enough to store his small treasure.

After using Margarita's body to take Héro, Bereft did not immediately return her body back to her apartment. Hers was an exquisite body that he possessed. It reminded him somewhat of a one-legged whore whom he had never had the chance to experience.

Bereft rarely took the time to reminisce over previous victims, but looking at the child from this corner of the room reminded him of the woman whom she might one day become.

When he took control of Margarita's body and accessed her memories, he marveled at some of the depravities this woman had already committed. Although she would never be able to fathom the delectable levels of atrocities her body was capable of, he had not entered the body and mind of one so deviant since the daughters of Hawwaa were given their names.

This woman, he thought, was strong of mind but she bent as easily to his will as if her own will were non-existent. Bereft drove back to the garage where Margarita kept her Jaguar. He checked the stars and could tell that the time was well beyond the midnight hour.

The young Hispanic man who came to the car door as soon as Bereft pulled up to the garage was approximately twenty years of age. Bereft got out of the car and left the keys in the ignition. As he walked past the bronze young man, Bereft could feel the boy's eyes caress this body that was now his. He turned in amusement. Oh, how many times he had played this game—giving the bodies of kings and queens to their slaves to do with as they wanted.

Bereft stared into the man-boy's soul through his eyes and saw his true desire. It was a boy's dream, simple and contrite. Bereft would grant him his desire and perhaps a bit more. He plucked the boy's name from Margarita's memory and called to him.

"Carlos."

"Yes, Miss Smith, there is something else I can do for you?"

Bereft walked back toward the car where Carlos was seated behind the steering wheel. The car door was still open and Bereft walked right in between the door and the car. Margarita's hips were wide, but still small enough to wriggle into the close space.

Bereft did not answer the man-boy. He kept the hips that he possessed six inches from Carlos's face where he knew they would have his desired effect. Bereft stood there for a moment and willed the pheromones of

Margarita's body to release into the air in front of Carlos, making it virtually impossible for Carlos to do anything but tremble as the scent of the woman in front of him coursed through his senses.

"There is something you can help me with, Carlos."

Bereft lifted the skirt that clung to Margarita's hips up to her waist to expose her perfectly trimmed pubic mound.

Carlos gasped at the sight of Margarita's perfectly pouting pussy lips. He had bragged to his friends on many occasions how the rich women whose cars he parked all begged him to fuck them. He would go on in detail about how he bent them over their own car hoods and took them from behind, making them beg for more.

His friends all knew the stories were only visions that he conjured in his own imagination, but they listened intently anyway, knowing that afterward they would tell a lie of their own, generously borrowing from Carlos' fantasies. Tomorrow they certainly wouldn't believe this.

Carlos was frozen behind the steering wheel. Bereft chuckled aloud at the absurdity of the man-boy's fear.

"You want to touch it, don't you, Carlos?"

Carlos could not find his voice and simply nodded.

"Well, here it is. Just for you. You want to stick a finger inside, like you do with your girlfriend, don't you?"

Carlos nodded again, still unable to grasp the reality of his good luck. He looked up from where he sat in the car and watched Miss Smith reach down with her free hand and wantonly splay her pussy lips for his perusal. Carlos looked around the garage from where he sat. If management were to see what was going on, he would be fired for sure. They were in the back of the garage where no one else could see them, he convinced himself as he felt his hand involuntarily rise to touch the beautiful venus in front of him.

Carlos touched the inner folds of Margarita's opening, felt her bear down, and engulfed the whole middle finger of his left hand before he could change his mind.

"Is this what you thought it would feel like, Carlos?" Bereft teased him using Margarita's most sultry voice. Bereft could see the man-boy's hardness in his pants and teased him further.

"You want to take your cock out, don't you, Carlos? Why don't you take it out and let me see it?"

Carlos shook his head no and continued to finger Margarita's vagina. There were only two women who had ever seen Carlos's penis, one was his mother and the other was his girlfriend. He knew it was a very small penis for a grown man, being only four inches long when fully erect, and was embarrassed to expose himself to anyone other than his virginal girlfriend who had never seen any penis except his.

"Take it out, Carlos," he heard Miss Smith say and he could not stop himself as he undid his zipper, pulled his underwear to the side, and let his tiny penis out through the opening of his pants.

The sound of Margarita's laughter when his penis came into view incensed Carlos. His girlfriend had only ever let him put one finger inside of her and now he maliciously pushed a second finger into Margarita. When he felt her vagina clamp down hard on his two fingers and saw the juices ooze onto his hand, he had to use his other hand to squeeze the head of his penis to keep it from squirting onto his pants. It was painful to him, but he had used the same trick when he was fingering his girlfriend in her mother's living room.

"Carlos, are you trying to keep that sweet juice from me? Come on, little boy, put another finger in me."

Bereft allowed the vagina that he now controlled to go slack so that Carlos could feel the extra space that was yet to be filled.

"Put two more fingers in if you want. See how easily I can take it."

The two extra fingers that Carlos put into Margarita were quickly soaked with the flow of secretions that her body was expelling.

Carlos was still nervous and still couldn't believe what was happening to him. He kept trying to look past Miss Smith and through the windshield to make sure that no one would come and discover what he was doing.

Bereft, on the other hand, couldn't care less. He was enjoying Margarita's body immensely. If there was such a thing, she was the perfect host, pliable, young, and with all the physical attributes of an Olympian athlete. It was a shame he had to leave this body soon. Any other time this body would have lasted him at least a week.

Carlos was pumping the four fingers of his left hand into Margarita faster than he had ever done with one finger inside his girlfriend. He was surprised when she kicked the shoe off of her right foot and brought her beautifully pedicured toes to brush against his thigh. Miss Smith kicked his hand away from his penis and brought her toes down on the little cock.

"Don't stop moving your hand." Carlos had to be reminded as he lost himself in the feeling of having his cock massaged between Margarita's big toe and her second toe. When she spoke he was startled out of a hazy euphoria and saw that she was balancing herself on one foot while simultaneously getting fucked by his hand and giving him a foot job. She wasn't even holding on to the side of the car.

Carlos felt himself about to come.

"Miss, Miss."

Bereft reached into the car and grabbed the back of Carlos's head. With his hand still filling her vaginal opening, Carlos's face was added to Bereft's pleasure. Carlos could not remove his hand as Miss Smith's vagina had locked down on it and now his lips were pressed against her clitoris. His girlfriend had never allowed him to perform this act on her, but he instinctively new where to suck.

Bereft's laugh was harsh as it came out in Margarita's voice. He felt the man-child's sticky fluids splatter onto Margarita's foot and decided it was time to finish. Bereft released Carlos's hand from Margarita's vagina and it made a loud slurping noise as the last finger was extracted from her hole. Bereft forced the man-boy's face lower until his mouth was against the now vacant opening and pushed his face forcefully into it. He ground the cunt that he possessed viciously against Carlos's face. Carlos tried frantically to gather the juices that poured out of Miss Smith into his mouth, but could not lick or suck fast enough to keep up with the flow of the thick fluid.

Bereft spent himself in a final heave against Carlos's face in time to avoid suffocating Carlos in an engorged vagina.

The man-boy was almost unconscious, but he was still lucid enough to notice the foot that was held up to his mouth. He could smell the acrid and pungent odor of his own sperm and knew what he was expected to do.

"Open up, boy. Isn't this what you wanted me to do?"

It tickled Bereft to no end that he had pulled the memory of another young man eating sperm from this same foot from Margarita's memory. Oh, if he only had more time with this one. If only he had more time.

Everything had its time and everything had its place. Up until a day ago he was sure of it. Now he was not so sure. At the least, there was more at risk than he had first thought. A new power had come into play. The old woman knew who and what he was, of that he was positive. His was a power that came from humanity's lack of knowledge of how to protect themselves from him.

Since Sodom, he was left with the handicap of being bound by salt, the most common of all the elements. He cursed the angels that laid him so low and for so long with their decree and spit at the taste of bile that set in his mouth at the memory of the Host of Hosts' army.

The old woman would come for him, he was sure of that. He would have to start building more of his own alliances to deal with her. The occupants of this building would not be up to the task. He would need to order his immediate intermediary to assign his lackeys the task of killing her before she found him. She was beyond his personal reach. He had felt her power even before the salt she poured on him touched him. It was akin to Chemah's power except that it had the strength of her knowledge attached. With that knowledge she could easily cause his destruction.

Bereft took a last long look at the sleeping child. She looked too comfortable and he had the urge to kick her, but that would have been beneath even him.

He opened the door to leave and came face to face with Big Tony, the leader of the drug gang in the area. The bigger man was about to knock on the door before it was opened and now that he saw the man within for the first time, he put his hand down immediately and took a step back.

Big Tony was the only one of his own gang who knew what Bereft was and what he could do. Bereft had made himself known to Big Tony after he'd done away with the rival drug gang.

For years, even before Tony had become the gang's leader, his predecessor tried to take Sangre Grande from their rivals and had failed at every attempt. When the streets started talking and announced that Big Tony had taken out all the major players in the opposing drug gang, Tony had not denied it. Instead he let everyone believe that it was true. It added to his street cred when the news announced that a police officer had been blamed for the murders. Days later he came to claim Sangre Grande and was met by Bereft.

Bereft showed him his power by entering one after another of Tony's minions without them knowing what had transpired. Bereft did things to the bodies that he possessed that made Tony cringe in fear, and the gang leader gave his allegiance in return for his own safety.

"Just checking to see if everything is alright."

"I have a job for you." Bereft ignored Tony's deference to him.

Bereft walked past him and Tony followed him down the stairs and out of the building. Tony's boys gave him a nod as he left the building behind the younger man they had let in the day before. He nodded back at them, but still listened carefully to all of the instructions that Bereft continued to give as he walked a short, but healthy distance behind the young man that Bereft now assumed. They reached the avenue and Bereft turned to Tony.

"When next we meet I may be in the guise of a woman. Will you know me?"

"I'll know you."

"How will you know me?"

"By your eyes."

"Yes, my eyes. They never change."

"You ain't never lie."

"No, I ain't never." Bereft turned and melted into the crowd of pedestrians walking in the same direction.

***

Michelle had no problem with Margarita, although their first encounter with each other two years before had not gone well. Margarita announced unequivocally that she was back on the scene and that she wanted her family back. Michelle did not back down at that time and each woman had gained a certain respect for the other. It didn't hurt their relationship any that Margarita had willingly saved Michelle's life. They weren't great friends, but the times when Margarita was forced to come to the house to either pick Héro up or drop her off, Michelle always invited her in. Strangely, if Tatsuya was home she would never accept the invitation to come in. It was almost as if she was afraid of him. For his part, Tatsuya never spoke to her or of her. When speaking to his little sister, he always referred to Margarita as, "your mother."

If Chemah was home he would always answer the door and let Héro in or out to her mother, but he was never cordial and he never let her past the threshold of the door.

That was why, when Margarita came to the door this morning with Héro's godmother, Kat, and Chemah invited her into the living room, it startled Michelle.

Tatsuya was not home. When they reached home from the hospital he told his father that he had to meet one of his friends around the corner and he jetted out of the house before Chemah could tell him what time to be home for dinner. Michelle wished he were here now. Suddenly she felt like she needed an ally.

Kat stepped through the door first and Margarita demurely stepped in after her. Very few things had changed in the living room that Margarita had decorated. The couch was new and a few new Charles Bibbs paintings were up on either side of the mantel. Margarita stepped close to one of them trying to inconspicuously figure out whether they were the originals

Chapter 20

Two Face

Michelle was feeling exceptionally well this Saturday morning. Before leaving the hospital earlier the doctor told her that she could come in either tomorrow or Monday to take the bandages off. He would leave it up to her.

He explained that the solution that he put in her eyes was the only thing that should be keeping her from seeing right away. A necessary antibiotic, the eye drops would dissolve into her eyes after a day. Thereafter, she would take the medication orally and she wouldn't miss another day of sight.

"Uh, yeah, I'll wait an extra day to see the world again." The sarcasm made her appear angry. "I'll be seeing you tomorrow, Doctor."

"I guess you will," the doctor said, chuckling at his own little joke. Michelle appreciated his attempt and came right back at him.

"Hey, leave the jokes to me, will you, Doc? You don't see me on stage holding a guy's balls and asking him to cough, do you? Well, maybe once, but I thought he was a midget with big cheeks choking on a chicken bone."

She was prepared when Chemah grabbed her roughly by the elbow and almost dragged her out of the doctor's office. He knew that the more nervous or anxious Michelle got, the raunchier her jokes would get. He loved her for her humor, but was always afraid that others wouldn't appreciate it. He almost always unnecessarily got embarrassed for her.

or limited-edition prints. No one saw her roll her eyes when she realized that the paintings were originals.

Probably bought with my money, she thought.

"My God, what a beautiful set of Charles Bibbs paintings," she said when she turned back to Chemah.

"Thank you," Michelle said from her seat by the bay window at the front of the living room. Margarita had not seen her sitting there and turned toward her voice.

"I purchased them years ago before I lost my sight. The Brian Branche behind you used to be my favorite."

Margarita turned to look behind her and saw an oil painting of what appeared to be a winged man emerging from a cloud of fire. The fire itself had a face and the man's wings seemed endless.

"It's called *The Fire Bird*. It was the last piece of art I bought before my sight went. It reminded me of the free spirit that I thought I was back then. Chemah thinks that it's still a good representation of my inner self." Michelle clutched her breast in an exaggerated theatrical gesture.

"Unfortunately, I can barely remember what it looks like. Every time I try to picture it in my mind the figure changes. Sometimes he's flying away gracefully, and other times I see him exploding out of arms that are trying to hold him back."

Margarita looked at the picture thoughtfully and thought that either one of the depictions could be quite accurate.

"What do you see, Margarita?"

"Oh, I'm not a big art connoisseur. I wouldn't know what to make of it."

Both Kat and Chemah, who had been admiring the painting that Michelle was discussing, turned to Margarita in astonishment. If there was anyone who knew about art, it was definitely Margarita. She owned a Charles Bibbs original of her own as well as a few Panchito oils and two Leroy Campbells that Chemah was aware of. They had been displayed in this same living room until their divorce was finalized. They were a few treasures that she won in the settlement.

Margarita was indeed aware of Brian Branche's art. She was actually a fan. She didn't have a work of his yet as Maya Angelou had outbid her for one that she was most interested in.

"Well, I guess it doesn't matter much as I'll be able to see it again as of tomorrow."

Margarita turned her full attention to the woman sitting in the shadow of the far side of the room, and took a few steps toward her.

"How's that?"

"Tomorrow. I'll be able to see again as of tomorrow. I thought you knew."

Michelle was well aware that no one but her family knew that she was getting her eyesight back. She and Chemah had discussed that no one should know what she was having done until they were sure that she would regain her sight. They had told everyone that they were vacationing in Europe when she had the operation in Israel, and the next operation was a two-day stint in the hospital during which her absence from the house would never have to be explained. Margarita had not even thought twice about it when Chemah told her earlier that he and Tatsuya were driving home with Michelle from the hospital.

Margarita took another step and finally saw that Michelle was wearing bandages over her eyes.

"You've had an operation?"

Kat came forward. After the discussion that she and Margarita just had back at Margarita's apartment, she was leery of what her friend might say or do.

"My God, Michelle, that is wonderful news!" Margarita said.

Margarita took another step toward Michelle.

"You've had an operation and you didn't tell anyone that you'd be able to see again?"

"Well, no one was sure that the first operation was a success until the second procedure was finished yesterday. The doctor says that the stem cells they used to grow new retina have attached perfectly and the scarred remnants of my retina came away, leaving no damage to the new ones."

"So you kept it to yourselves?" Margarita turned to Chemah.

Chemah understood why Michelle was always so uncharacteristically cordial with Margarita. She did, after all, save Michelle's life. However, he felt no such compunction.

"We didn't think it was anybody else's business but our own."

"I see. So the fact that my daughter's father's lover, who is living with him outside the sanctity of marriage—"

Kat put her hand on Margarita's shoulder, but Margarita shrugged it off.

"No, I'm going to say it. Who is shacking up with him, showing my daughter no respect, and being no example of how respectable women behave, is going to be seeing her for the first time is not something I should know about? I beg to differ."

"You can beg all you want and it's not going to make a damn bit of difference. Despite our not being married, Michelle is a great role model for Héro. She teaches her the value of hard work, respect for adults and, I might add, perseverance." Chemah's voice softened. "Things that I know for certain, from listening to Héro talk about what you and she do together, that you reinforce every moment of time that you spend with her."

Then his voice got hard again. "But I will not let you stand here and talk to and about Michelle in that manner. And if you can't understand that, then you can leave my house right now."

"*Your* house!"

Kat put her hand on Margarita's shoulder again. This time Margarita heeded her warning. The thought of losing her hard-earned home always pissed her off, but she knew she was treading on thin ice.

"Okay. All I'm saying is that, like you said a moment ago, if I'm going to reinforce all of the wonderful things that you two are doing here at home with Héro, then maybe I should be let in on some of the happenings around here. That's all."

Chemah listened to Margarita and marveled at how she could still use someone else's own words to manipulate a situation in her favor.

"We'll keep that in mind for the next time, Margarita, but in the meantime, Héro isn't here right now, is she?"

A somber quiet filled the room. Kat looked uncomfortable and Margarita shifted from one leg to the other. Michelle faced the closed window again as if she could see something out there that no one else could, and Chemah cursed.

"Fuck!"

Margarita shifted her feet again.

"Let's not do this right now, Margarita. If we have anything more to say to each other let's say it after we find Héro."

Chemah walked to the table at the far side of the room that was littered with paper. He picked up a pile of paper that stood about six inches high and brought it back to where Kat and Margarita stood.

"You came here to help, right? Well, this is how you can help. Take these and post them everywhere you can, from One Hundred Thirtieth Street and St. Nicholas Avenue to One Hundred Tenth Street and Fifth Avenue."

Margarita took the stack of papers and took a look at the page at the top of the pile. It was a photo of Héro. Under it was written, REWARD FOR ANY INFORMATION LEADING TO FINDING THIS GIRL $2,000,000.00.

Margarita stared at the dollar amount in shock. She had given Chemah $1.5 million in their divorce settlement when the consultancy firm bought her out of her partnership. Margarita had given the money gladly knowing that Chemah would use it to treat her daughter like a princess while she was away in the penitentiary.

"Where are you going to get all of this money?"

"I have the money. The one-point-five million that you gave me for Héro has been in a high-yielding investment account since the day that you signed it over to me. I check how it's doing every other month or so. As of yesterday it's yielded about half a million dollars within the past four years, give or take a few thousand dollars."

"You put everything into this? All the money that you have?"

"Not everything. There's still the house. If I have to sell it to get Héro back I'll do it. That's probably another two million, right?"

Margarita nodded her head. She knew the market value of the house. For the first time since Héro disappeared Margarita began to cry. It started out as a sob, choked back by her fear of emoting in public. Then the tears started to rain down her face and she couldn't stop the uncontrollable weeping, sobbing, and sniffling as the pain of losing her only child finally racked her body, contorting Margarita into a hunched over uncontrollable mess.

Kat tried to hold her up and console her, but it did no good. Margarita was trembling and convulsing so much that Chemah thought she would hurt herself at any moment.

Kat looked to Chemah, but he was already on his way to her.

"It's going to be alright. We're going to find her," he lied while trying to pull Margarita upright. Margarita allowed Chemah to straighten her back, but was not able to stifle the sobs. She knew the truth as well as he did and the desperation of the flyers finally brought it all home. The truth was that the longer Héro was missing, the less likely they were to find her. It had already been more than two weeks since she was taken.

Margarita spoke in between sobs.

"I didn't do enough. I didn't give any money. You gave everything and I didn't think to give my last dollar to get my baby back."

"You did everything that you could, Margarita." Chemah held her to his chest and rubbed her back.

Margarita pushed away from Chemah.

"Stop saying that." Margarita wiped her eyes with the back of her hand. "It's not true and you know it. I sat back and let everyone else do what I should have done. I should have been the one to offer two million dollars for her return. I should have offered five million. I should have been walking the pavement asking everyone and anyone if they had seen her. Me. Her mother." Margarita broke into another fit of crying, but was controlled enough now that she was attempting to wipe her own tears as they poured out of her.

Chemah felt genuinely sorry for her. After all this time Margarita was finally able to come in contact with some real feelings of her own. It was a shame that the cost of this epiphany was the loss of their daughter.

Chemah came to her again and held her by both shoulders.

"We are going to find her, Margarita, I promise."

Margarita sniffled. Dejected and beaten, she looked as if she were on the verge of breaking down again. When Chemah shook her again gently, she looked into his eyes and threw her arms around his neck, burying her face in his shoulder. He stroked the back of her head until she quieted again and then she seemed to come totally to her senses.

"Thank you, Chemah, for everything. Now Kat and I have work to do."

Margarita scrambled to pick the flyers up from where she'd dropped them on the floor. Kat came over to help her, taking half the pile that had fallen under her arm.

Margarita reached the front door and opened it. On second thought, she looked back at the painting on the wall titled *The Fire Bird* and turned back to Michelle, who was still facing the window.

"Michelle, that Brian Branche piece, I think it symbolizes a rebirth, a new start. Maybe even a coming of age. That's what I get from it, anyway." Margarita held the door open for Kat and they walked out together. Chemah came behind them and closed the door, securing the bottom lock before coming back into the living room.

"Chemah, do you really think that you're going to find Héro after all this time?"

"I don't know anymore, but I'm not giving up. I'm not going back to work until I find her, one way or another."

Michelle understood what he meant by "one way or another." Until now she hadn't known that he was dealing with that part of the reality of Héro's disappearance. Chemah was always so closed up, and kept his true thoughts and feelings locked inside himself. He never let anyone, including her, know what he was thinking.

"Are you going to go out again. I mean, do you have any new leads?"

"Nothing. The reward hasn't even brought us any fake leads. I posted it on the Internet yesterday and got about fifty or so hits. I checked them all out, nothing credible to look into. Pretty soon I'm going to have to start looking into the incredible."

"After tomorrow I'll be able to help you keep looking. I won't do anything else until we get her back. One way or another."

Chemah came over to where she was by the window and kissed her on the forehead. He saw Margarita and Kat get into the Jaguar and thought he should check for email responses again before doing the flyer distribution on the east side that he intended. If she were still alive, it was possible that Héro was already very far away. A number of children who were found after being abducted, were located far from their homes just as many as were found dead close by. Maybe some good samaritan would see her and get in contact, he prayed.

"I'm going to work upstairs for a while. Do you need anything?"

"Base probably needs some water. He's been in the backyard all morning."

"I'll get him some," Chemah said, heading for the kitchen.

A minute later Chemah came back into the living room.

"He's gone."

"Who's gone?"

"Base."

"What do you mean he's gone? Is there a hole under the fence? Did he tunnel underneath?"

"No, his leash is gone too."

"Tatsuya took him?"

"Probably. I'll go look for them. Base has probably bitten somebody by now."

"Don't worry so much about them. Tatsuya can handle him pretty well by now. He's probably chasing the other kids up and down the block with him. You know how kids are. Anyhow, Base has never bitten a kid."

"Yeah, not yet he hasn't. I told that kid before that he couldn't take Base out by himself. Damn it, he's not listening to me anymore."

Michelle did not want to say anything, but maybe now was the right time.

"You have been spending a lot of time looking for Héro. You guys used to hang together all the time. Maybe he just needs a little more attention."

Chemah was headed up the stairs to use the bathroom before going out to look for his son, but stopped and came back down.

"Did he say something to you?"

"No, but he didn't have to. I can tell he misses his sister as much as you miss your daughter. You've all been inseparable since the day she was born. He probably blames himself for her abduction as much as you do. He was right there. Baby, that's a lot for a little boy to be holding on to. The other night I heard him talking in his sleep. He was saying Héro's name over and over."

"He told me he was having dreams about her, but I didn't think it was that bad."

Michelle faced the sun coming through the window again. "Go find him. Talk to him. You're really all the family he's got right now."

Chemah was going to remind her that she was family too, but thought he would only be stating the obvious. He turned back to the stairs, heading for the bathroom again.

"I'll bring him home and talk to him. Shit, I hope that dog hasn't bitten anyone. If he has you're going to pay for it," he said half jokingly.

Michelle didn't answer him. She was daydreaming about being reborn and flying again.

‡‡‡

Margarita and Kat sat in the car together for a moment before Margarita turned the ignition.

"So what did you think?"

"I thought it was the greatest performance by one of the greatest bitches of all time."

"You knew?"

"Wasn't sure till now. Marge, how could you?"

Margarita held herself back from even getting involved in a dispute about Kat calling her Marge. Margarita knew that Kat knew, full well, she hated being called "Marge." She knew Kat used it when she was angry with her, to make sure she had Margarita's full attention. It was a mind game only a best friend could play.

"All that shit you put down in there was fake?"

"Only the tears were fake. The emotion was real. I should have been the one who put up the money. I'm mad at myself about that. But he did put his arms around me and damn if it didn't feel good again."

"Marge, if he finds out that you were faking that cry, you know what he'll do?"

"How's he going to find out? You're the only one who knows. You know damn well I'm not going to get a bout of the confessional blues."

Margarita put the car into drive and turned to Kat expectantly.

"Well?"

"I'm not getting involved in your mess again. But I'm not going to jail for your ass either. I better not even think that you're going to go fuck with that blind girl."

"What blind girl? You heard her. As of tomorrow she is in the land of the sighted again."

"You know what I mean."

"Yeah, I know what you mean and you don't have to worry. The only thing I'm concerned with right now is my baby girl. Thinking about her alone in the world is the only thing that kept me alive that whole time I was sitting in jail. God, if I ever find out who took her I'll have their balls cut off."

"Now that's the Margarita I know. Let's get going. After we hang these flyers, I told my mother we were going to stop by the church. Her whole congregation is saying a prayer for my goddaughter."

Margarita was deeply touched. She had all but forgotten about the church. If her mother were alive, it would have been the first thing she would have called for. The thought of her own mother sent a wave of serenity through her that she had not felt in a long time. Margarita reached over her bucket seat to Kat and gave her a bear hug and a kiss.

"Is that a real tear in your eye, or am I the mark now?"

"Oh fuck you, bitch."

"Mmmm-hmmm. That's what I thought. We better get to church quick. You need Jesus in your life."

"You sound just like your mother."

"I know. I sound like everybody's mother these days."

Margarita couldn't agree more.

Chapter 21

Blessings

"—but why is he after my father?"

Lydia didn't want to alarm Tatsuya, but she didn't want to lie to him either. It was important that he know what they were going up against before she involved him in her plan. Lydia decided that total candor with the boy was her only recourse. But as grounded and smart as Tatsuya was she wasn't sure he would be able to accept the unbelievably supernatural nature of the only explanation she could give.

"In the beginning God is said to have created three types of beings. Angels made from the air, Men made from the earth, and the Djinn were made from fire. Tatsuya, the entity that is after jour father is a Djinn. Do you know what a Djinn is?"

Tatsuya was aware of his new friend's accent and he thought that she pronounced it wrong.

"Do you mean a genie, like in Aladdin?"

Lydia was glad that Tatsuya had a reference to gather from, but the Aladdin animation was not what she wanted him to think of when he thought of a Djinn.

"The word *genie* does come from the word *Djinn*, but still *Djinn* is the appropriate word to use. Some time ago someone decided to change the name because they were not used to hearing the word in their language. The word *Djinn* comes from the Middle East where Islam is practiced. *Djinn* is the word that Islam gave these entities, but they have been known in many forms to the entire world."

"You mean there's more than one Djinn?"

"Oh, there are many many Djinns in the world. For the most part they live among humans doing whatever it is they want to do. Some are good and some are very mischievous, but only a few are evil. Unfortunately the Djinn that is attracted to jour father is very evil."

"Why does he want to hurt Dad and why did he take Héro?"

Lydia took the leash that Tatsuya held in his hand and yanked it a little causing Base to come to stand on all fours again.

"Let's start walking. I'll tell you everything on the way."

Tatsuya had been warned by his father not to talk to strangers, but this was the woman who had talked to him in his dreams. She even looked liked the doll that Héro played with in the house where all the blood was spilled. When Base didn't bite her immediately, Tatsuya decided it was okay to follow her. Lydia reached back and tried to take Tatsuya's hand as they made their way to the first corner. Tatsuya looked at Lydia's hand and tried to act as if he did not see it.

"Don't jou think jour father would want jou to help an old lady cross the street?"

Tatsuya could see Lydia's point, but still looked up and down the street to make sure that none of his friends were coming. They wouldn't understand what was going on and would tease him endlessly when he was hanging out on the block. Tatsuya and Lydia walked another block before Tatsuya thought to let go of her hand again. By that time he was already to another corner and thought it would be easier to hold her hand as long as Lydia thought she needed him to.

"So why did the genie take Héro?" Tatsuya demanded from Lydia.

"You mean the Djinn."

Tatsuya nodded that he heard her. Lydia stopped walking and looked at Tatsuya gravely.

"No, Tatsuya, say it. I need to know that jou do not think this is some Disney cartoon that we are dealing with. Say the name properly."

"The Djinn. Why is the Djinn after my father? Why did he take Héro?"

Lydia seemed to be satisfied with Tatsuya's pronunciation of the name and was now ready to answer all of his questions.

"Have you ever noticed that jour father does special things that no one else does?"

"Special, like what?

"Maybe he sees things that no one else does, or knows things that no one else knows."

Tatsuya smiled that someone besides him knew this about his father.

"Dad can always tell when something is about to happen. He says that if I keep training my karate, that I'll be just like him."

"Yes, well, jou are going to be like him if jou do jour karate or not. People like me or beings like the Djinn can see this clearly. There is an aura of power that shines brightly in your Dad. Although it is only a small spark in jou right now, one day jour aura will burn like a roaring flame. I will make sure of this, as I have let the power that should have been jour father's go without training, I will not make the same mistake with jou."

Tatsuya was a little scared at Lydia's prediction, but was still fascinated.

"This Djinn, if all of my information is correct, is named Bereft. He sees in your father the power that he coveted many centuries ago from one of God's chosen children. That is, one of the men that God chose to grant power to, power like those granted to the angels. This power cannot be taken from a being like your father. It is a power that can only be given by He who possesses it. Jour father does not know the extent of this power because I chose wrongly not to teach him. A being like Bereft, however, would turn this power inside out. He would corrupt it and make himself whole. Whole like no other being has ever been. He would be of all three worlds, born of fire, earth, and air. Bereft believes that then he'll finally be able to talk to God the way that men and angels have been known to do."

Tatsuya was amazed by all of this information and it showed on his face. Lydia thought she should give him information that he would find easier to digest.

"But he knows that jour father loves his children above all else and would be driven to distraction to find Héro and eventually give anything to have her back."

"He's going to take Dad's power?"

"Unfortunately, to take his power, his body must also be taken. Your father will never be your father again if he allows this. That is why we must hurry to get Héro back home."

Tatsuya was very worried before he had this information. Now he felt a greater urgency than he had ever felt. Tatsuya reached for the leash that held Base and Lydia relinquished it. She sensed that the dog made him feel safer.

Chapter 22

The Powers that Be

Lydia was bringing Héro down the last flight of stairs of the Sangre Grande building when Big Tony came running down the stairs behind them at full speed. He had a nine in his left hand and a Desert Eagle in his right. When he saw it was Lydia holding Héro's hand, he stopped in his tracks. He knew this woman, had known her for years. Like every other criminal bound for jail he was superstitious. His mother had sent him to this woman many years ago to be cleansed of any evil spirits before he went to court for sentencing. He did two years on that bid, but it could have been fifteen to life. He felt grateful to the woman and sent his mother back to her to make an offering.

"Old woman, I can't let you take that little girl."

Lydia and Héro turned simultaneously. Héro smiled at him. He had been very nice to her. He brought her a new toy and food everyday. Only he wouldn't take her back to her father or mother when she asked him. She frowned when she thought about that and the look on her face scared Big Tony. He didn't know what to expect from one minute to the next and for all he knew, the little girl's displeasure could cause his death. The powerful old santera's presence here was a sure sign that he was dealing with things that he had no business being involved in.

"Anthony, it's a long time that I no see jou."

All of a sudden Big Tony was self-conscious about the gun he held in each hand. There was nowhere to put them where they would not be seen, so he let them hang impotently at his sides.

"Old woman, I can't let you—"

"Jou can't let me what? Take the baby? Jou are not letting me take her? Jou are putting her in my care."

The old santera let go of Héro's hand and took a step toward Big Tony. The sudden move scared him and his hands came up, pointing both guns at Lydia.

Lydia stopped in her tracks and took a curious look up and down the length of Big Tony's body. She smiled after a moment and took Héro's hand again.

"Jou are still a good boy, Anthony. Let us out of here and jou can still receive many blessings. Jou have no killed anyone jet." The santera started out of the building again.

Big Tony's reputation was built on the myth that he was a notorious killer, but the old woman was right. He had never actually killed anyone. That she knew his secret lent strength to her position and Big Tony let the guns fall to his sides again. He would plead with the santera before he would raise the guns again and do what he had to.

"Old lady, please—don't make me—"

This time the santera turned around and there was a dark flame in her eyes.

"Jou know me by name, Anthony, and I know what will or what will not become of jou this night. *Por favor*, do not be disrespectful again."

The santera's voice was ominous and every word she spoke disarmed Big Tony with its veiled warnings.

"An old friend of jours needs jou tonight. We have to hurry or he will fall to the evil one that would be jour master."

Big Tony's face showed surprise that she knew his plight.

"Of course, I know. Jou estupey? For what jou think I am doing here?"

It only took Big Tony a moment to make his decision. He thought about dropping the guns and going with the santera and then thought better of leaving the guns. He tucked them both in the back of his pants and pulled his shirt over them to conceal them from view. If all else failed he would use one of them to kill himself.

The santera looked over her shoulder and winked at Big Tony as she opened the door to let them all out into the street.

"Don't worry, jou won't have to kill jourself."

Outside the building, Tatsuya had the one skinny teenager who was left as a lookout in front of the building hemmed up in a corner of the stoop by the concrete gargoyle ornament that obstructed the entrance. Base wasn't barking, but he was emitting a low humming growl from the bottom of his fang-filled mouth that pleaded with Tatsuya to let the leash go.

When Tatsuya and Héro saw each other they both screeched with joy. Tatsuya almost let the leash go trying to get to Héro, but caught it and pulled it back just as Base jumped at the cringing teenager. He had to hold the leash with two hands now and struggled to pull Base to where Héro stood. Still holding the leash, he bent and put his arm around his sister. They were able to hug each other for a moment before they heard the gravity in Lydia's voice.

"Let's hurry away from here, children. We have to get home to jour father."

Big Tony walked over to where the skinny teenager was composing himself.

"Where did Bud and Fingers go?"

"Said they was going to Jimbo's to get some eats. They told me to wait for them here."

"Let them know I was looking for them. If they're not standing in front of this building when I get back—"

Big Tony shrugged. And the teenager knew what that meant. It was likely the two men would know what it meant too.

The skinny teenager's eyes followed Big Tony and the rest of the small group as they moved quickly down the block. He saw Tony jump quickly out of the way as the dog the little boy was walking with jumped at him. It made him feel better to know he wasn't the only one afraid of dogs.

Chapter 23

KRYPTONITE

When the doorbell rang it startled Chemah. He'd literally just walked into the house and closed the door behind him when the bell sounded. Chemah hadn't seen nor felt anyone close behind him. He hoped it was Tatsuya. Chemah had gone around the block twice searching for Tatsuya and Base before deciding to go home and wait for them at the house.

"Did you find them, Chemah?" Michelle called out.

"No." Chemah opened the door without checking the peephole and found an unpleasant surprise outside.

"Captain Brea, what are you doing here?"

There was never an occasion when one cop dropped in on another unannounced at their home. It was a standard rule of conduct in the department that everyone adhered to, as no one liked to bring their work home with them.

The captain looked different. *Maybe he's been out drinking.* Chemah searched for a reason to have his boss standing at his doorway.

"Are you going to invite me in?"

"Who is it, Chemah?"

Before Chemah could invite him in, Captain Brea was already stepping through the doorway.

"It's my boss, honey."

The captain looked around the house as if he were expecting something different, but didn't say anything.

"You mean the asshole that's been riding you for no reason, hon?"

"That's the one, dearest, right here in our home."

Chemah wasn't the type who approved of such blatant disrespect, but this was Michelle's home as much as his and she had the right to voice her opinion. At least he could soften some of her antics if he couldn't mute her voice.

Chemah never took his eyes off the captain. He was in no mood for his bullshit. He told him in the office that he wasn't coming back to work until he found his daughter, and he hoped that the captain wasn't here trying to get him to change his mind again.

"Do you know what cancer is?"

"Excuse me, Captain Brea, but I don't think you should be here right now. My wife and I were about to go."

"This body has cancer. I've never felt anything like it before," Captain Brea slurred.

The captain has been drinking, Chemah thought.

"Captain Brea, why don't you let me call you a cab?"

The captain walked over to where Michelle was sitting, but Chemah managed to step between him and Michelle before he could reach her. The captain laughed an ugly laugh and then stopped suddenly.

"I could touch her if I wanted to, you know? I mean, I could really touch her."

Michelle got up from her seat behind Chemah.

"You go ahead and try to touch me, motherfucker. Let's see how bad you want it."

Chemah knew she already had the box cutter in her hand. Michelle was attacked in her apartment a few years ago. Since that time, she went nowhere without it. Chemah had even seen her leave it on the sink while she was showering on occasion.

Chemah thought she was overreacting to the situation. The captain was obviously drunk and even though he and Chemah were at odds with each other, he was still Chemah's boss.

"Captain Brea, I think it's time that you leave."

Chemah placed his hand on his boss's shoulder and attempted to guide him toward the door. The captain allowed himself to be led for a few steps and then stopped in his tracks and forcefully shrugged Chemah's hand off.

"Tell me, God's light—what does it feel like to have your precious child taken from you?"

Chemah was taken aback by the captain's strange choice of words, but he got his meaning. Chemah didn't care how drunk the captain was; he was not going to let anyone disrespect the memory of his daughter. Chemah tried to grab the captain by the arm, but the captain pushed him away before he could grab hold of him.

"You see, but you don't see, God's light. Maybe this will help you understand."

The captain held out his open hand and in the middle of it was Héro's hair barrette. Chemah stood transfixed for a moment, looking at the small piece of plastic that his boss held extended toward him. Chemah reached for it and Captain Brea allowed him to snatch the tiny piece from his palm. Chemah stared at the barrette and in an instant his eyes were sharp with recognition.

"Good, you recognize it. The veil is finally lifted from your eyes and you begin to see. There is now one less blind person in the room."

"Chemah? Chemah? What is it?" Michelle was still standing and took a misstep toward Chemah's voice. She bumped into a chair and was able to right herself before inertia and disequilibrium could take her to the floor.

"It's nothing. Stay where you are," Chemah said without taking his eyes off of his boss.

Chemah watched Edwin Brea carefully as the man paced back and forth calmly as he spoke. Edwin Brea was not taking his eyes off Chemah either.

Chemah was reminded of a panther he saw at the zoo with Héro a few months ago. He and Héro had stared in awe at the giant cat. While Héro found the graceful cat mesmerizing, only Chemah knew that the cat wanted nothing more than to devour his audience. Only the thick glass kept him at bay. He had no clue what was holding Edwin Brea back, but with all of the talking that the captain was doing, Chemah knew that he was going to find out soon.

"Is he saying that he is holding Héro hostage? Is that what this devil is saying? No, no, no, noooo. Motherfucker, nooo."

Michelle now openly brandished the box cutter that she held and started to tear at the bandages on her face.

The title of "devil" was not lost on Bereft. It was bestowed upon him in many other languages and although it did not quite describe what he was by any means, he was insulted by its use.

"No, not a devil, Michelle," Bereft spoke over Chemah's shoulder. "I have been many things, but at the moment I am merely a merchant here on business. I want to make a trade—to barter, if the term is more suitable to you. I will give Héro back to you if Chemah gives himself to me."

"What do you mean give myself to you?" Chemah now knew that his boss had lost his mind. He was stalling for time in hopes that the crazy man would divulge where his daughter was.

"Let me see. How can I make myself clearer? Ahh, there."

Chemah watched as Edwin Brea walked over to the front doorway. He looked up to the eight-inch crucifix that was placed on the molding above the door and with little more than a hop Edwin Brea snatched the crucifix from its place. He only landed on the floor for a moment before effortlessly jumping again. This time he replaced the crucifix on the molding, but he placed it upside-down.

The ceilings in Chemah's living room were twelve feet high. He guessed that the molding was just two feet below the ceiling. It would have been an impressive feat for a professional basketball player to make. For a six-foot, two-hundred-and-fifty-pound man who claimed to have cancer to make the jump twice in four seconds without even breathing hard was unbelievable. Chemah made a note that he would not underestimate the physical strength of this man again.

"The symbol that the serial killer uses. You want me to find the serial killer? That's why you took Héro? It doesn't make sense. She was taken before you even knew about the symbol used by the serial killer...before you even knew there was a serial killer."

It didn't take Chemah long to deduce that Edwin Brea was lying. There was no way he could have taken Héro. He didn't fit the model that Chemah was looking for. He would have to be a master of disguise, unless he hired someone who could look like Margarita. Chemah went through all of the possibilities quickly in his head and kept coming up with the same thing. Captain Brea was bullshitting him. Detectives Rodriguez and Flores probably figured out what Chemah was looking at in the picture with the magnifying glass and told the captain about it. But where was the captain going with this charade?

"So you're saying that you want me to find the serial killer and then you'll give me Héro."

Bereft shook his head in disgust. *Could the God's light be so stupid*?

"I am he whom you claim to be looking for. I took the lives in Fallujah, in Israel, in the salted sea that was once Sodom, and in this fetid land called Harlem. It was I who played with the bones of the woman who traveled in the hollow craft that flies through the sky. It was I who came looking for you, God's light, and it is you who must willingly be mine."

"Holy shit, he's crazy!" Michelle gave voice to Chemah's thoughts. The gauze covering her eyes was gone and she was blinking a mile a minute, trying to make out the two dark and blurry figures in front of her.

Chemah stood stock still, not wanting to make any sudden moves that might trigger some other psychotic episode in this man.

"You don't believe my words, God's light? Then maybe you will believe your eyes. A gentle touch for Michelle should put you on the path to enlightenment."

Bereft took a step forward and Chemah blocked his path. There was no way he was going to let Captain Brea by him to get to Michelle. Bereft could see that Chemah would lay his life down before he would let him pass.

Michelle saw the dark blurry figure moving forward toward her and couldn't help but scramble back into the farthest corner of the room. She fell over a chair again, but was able to keep the box cutter in front of her so that she didn't cut herself as she breathed heavily and leaned against the wall at her back.

The shadowy figure farthest from her she now knew was Chemah's crazy boss. She couldn't make out his face, but she wasn't taking her eyes off him. She was realizing that the more she blinked, the sharper her focus became. Her sight was almost back.

"Very well. Let us take a walk along the road. The first person that we meet along the way will be a testament to my power and then you will see the futility of resisting me."

"Then you'll take me to see my daughter." Chemah played along with Edwin Brea's madness.

"If it be your last boon after you have agreed to open yourself to me. I may grant you a last look at your daughter."

"Okay, let's go."

Chemah didn't think it would be that easy to get him out of the house. His only strategy was to put as much space between Captain Brea and Michelle as he could. Once he got him outside the house, he knew that Michelle would call the police and they would send a patrol car around.

Chemah always put his gun away when he was at home. He now regretted it as he made out the outline of the gun that protruded under Edwin Brea's suit jacket. Chemah didn't even have a pair of handcuffs that he could use if an opportunity to subdue the captain presented itself.

Bereft opened the front door and arrogantly took the three steps down to the walkway. It only took him a moment to realize that something was amiss.

Chemah was still at the top of the stairs looking down at Edwin Brea when he felt someone coming up on his right side. He instinctively took a defensive posture. Out of the shadows on his right Chemah saw a familiar face staring at him. Chemah was about to greet him when he saw the man raise a yellow-and-red canister above his head and throw it. Before it left the man's hands Chemah was able to read the label on it—*Red Cross Salt.*

Chemah jumped out of the way, but realized that the canister was not meant to hit him. The white contents spilled out in front of the doorway to the house and Chemah was assaulted by a shout that nearly split his eardrum.

"AAAAAAAARRRRRRRRRRRGGGGGGHHHhhhhhhhh!"

It was Captain Brea. A pitiful wail escaped him after the initial shout, as he turned to the man who was still in the shadows. Chemah could see that the man had another canister of salt. He held it in front of him with the spout open and trickling salt as he scrambled down the stoop steps, scurrying to get past the captain. Chemah could swear that the man waving the salt canister like a gun was none other than his childhood friend Anthony Pone.

Bereft gave Big Tony a wide berth as Tony carefully made his way past him, trailing a salt path as he eased his way up the walk. "I'll see you soon," Bereft said to him as he passed.

"I'll see you in hell," Big Tony said, full of false bravado.

"That's a promise," Bereft said, blowing Big Tony a silent kiss.

Tony crossed himself three times and said a complete "Hail Mary" prayer before he reached the end of the walkway.

Chemah's eyes followed Big Tony all the way to the sidewalk where Chemah finally saw a silent little group standing and holding hands. It was Tatsuya, Héro, and Lydia Anglero. Chemah could see that Tatsuya was holding Base by the collar and not by the leash the way Chemah had shown him to whenever he wanted to keep the dog close. At the sight of Héro, Chemah came bounding down the stairs forgetting about the threat that Captain Brea had posed only moments ago.

If it weren't for Chemah's trained reflexes, his head would have been taken completely off his shoulders. The hand that hit him grazed his jaw, and Chemah felt the bone crack and split up the side of his face near his ear. He was flat on his back and Captain Brea jumped on him and straddled his hips, keeping Chemah's arms pinned to his side.

"So you believe that you are more clever than the Grand Schemer? Salt in front of your doorway so that I cannot enter again. Salt on all four sides of the path so that I cannot flee. All the while having me believe that you had not yet accepted or even recognized the power that stands before you, while you make good the escape of your daughter. Oh, you are a clever one for sure, God's light, but I wonder did you think what I might do if given no other means of egress? I may not be able to taste of the God light inside of you without your consent, but I can still strip your soul from your body and wear your skin like a wet shirt."

Bereft grabbed Chemah by a handful of locks and held Chemah's face close up to the one Bereft now wore.

"Do you hear me, God's light? I cannot die and your soul is forfeit."

***

Lydia Anglero had set the stage for this final battle and the fight she knew would be all hers. She knew Bereft was inside the house with Chemah when she instructed Big Tony to pour the thirty canisters of salt that they stopped at the supermarket to get liberally on all sides of the house and the walkway. It finally sealed the walkway with salt five feet away from the sidewalk where she would be watching and waiting for the part that she must play.

Big Tony was not a willing participant in this event. She lied to him on the way to the supermarket, where she made him pay for the salt and told him that Bereft would not be able to enter him while he wore the amulet that she made for him. She handed him a string of white beads that were as useless against Bereft as a baked potato and he grudgingly did what he was told. Lydia told him that he could leave after he fortified the front door with salt, and he was more than willing to run back to Sangre Grande after Bereft promised to see him again.

Lydia knew that Chemah would not be ready to fight Bereft. You had to believe in such a thing before you could commit to its destruction. She was sorry that she had not indoctrinated him into her school of beliefs as a child. In joining the police force he had followed his natural path as a fighter of evil and had armed himself as well as he could against those forces without even knowing that they existed. Lydia blamed herself for seeing such a power in a young man and not directing it appropriately. She could claim that she was also a novice at the time, but it was only an excuse. Now she saw the same power in his son and thought to correct her mistake.

Before coming into the box that the salt created for her would-be captive she told Tatsuya to take a step back and not to cross the threshold of the salt lines until she told him it was okay. She knew that Bereft could not enter the children, especially not Tatsuya. But he could still harm them physically and the physical threat toward one of the children would certainly be a weakness to her.

Bereft did not hear Lydia coming up behind him with the large bag of salt that she had in her arms. He was a moment away from killing Chemah, who was semi-conscious, when Lydia poured five pounds of salt directly on top of him. Bereft made a sound like a wounded animal and jumped off Chemah's body, which was now also covered in salt. He ran toward the side of the house, trying to escape the pain that came with staying inside Edwin Brea's salt-covered body. However, he was knocked backward by the invisible wall created by the salt that he was not capable of crossing. Bereft jumped to his feet again and tried running the opposite way, but was once again knocked backward by the invisible wall created by the well-placed salt. Edwin Brea's eyes were wild with fear and pain. He saw the children at the end of the walkway, each with a canister of salt in their hands. He only had one other chance. He had to get the burning salt off this body. Bereft rolled back and forth on the ground for a full thirty seconds in much the same way that burn victims were told to extinguish fire from their bodies. He knew that it was too late when he felt his essence begin to ooze from the lips of Edwin Brea. The last thing Bereft saw from Edwin's eyes was the black flame that Lydia Anglero's eyes held whenever she was doing her work. She scooped the black ooze into a salt-filled container careful not to let any of it touch her.

The stories of how Djinns were captured and stored in bottles were not so far from the truth. The Djinns, of which Bereft was one, were powerful entities that preyed upon the humans whose greed for lust and power left them open to possession. The Djinns were said to be jealous of the power that God bestowed upon the children of Adam and Eve so that they might someday come back to his light. The Djinns called this power "God light."

Chapter 24

Honey, is that You?

Michelle stood at the door of Chemah's hospital room just barely out of Chemah's and Lydia's sight.

Chemah's final encounter with Bereft left the detective seriously wounded. By the time Michelle was able to get out of the house in the aftermath, the police had already surrounded Chemah and he was being carried into the ambulance. Three burly officers charged with protecting the wounded detective were sitting in the back of the ambulance. Michelle had not been able to glimpse her lover even though her vision cleared to nearly 20/20.

Leaving the children with Mrs. Richmond, Michelle took a cab to St. Luke's Hospital. Normally, getting into a cab proved to be a major event as Michelle not only had to convince the driver that he wouldn't be attacked, but she had to control Base enough so that he couldn't get a fleshy snack. The whole convincing/controlling exercise usually took the entire trip. Although Michelle was very comfortable reacquainting herself with the freedom afforded with sight, moving around without Base still felt very awkward. Instead of looking for a sign that would direct her to the Information Desk, Michelle instinctively stopped a security guard who directed her to the second-floor east wing of the hospital. The police officers that guarded Chemah's room at the far end of the hall asked her to identify herself. They knew her name. She was on the very short list of people who would be allowed to see Chemah. The media were already clamoring for the story of a badly injured detective and a dead captain and tried to use different ploys to gain access. The two officers assured Michelle that Chemah was alright and that he already had a visitor as they stepped to each side of the door and allowed her to pass.

Michelle was actually seeing Chemah for the first time. *My God, he's beautiful!*

Insecurity made Michelle hesitate entering the room. Instead, she paused to listen to the conversation that was taking place.

"Did jou notice the eyes?"

Chemah's eyes had been wide with disbelief, but were now focused with the memory of Captain Brea's eyes.

"The eyes never change. No matter what body he takes the eyes are always his. The saying, '*the eyes are the windows of the soul,*' was penned after meetings with beings such as Bereft," Lydia explained further.

As unbelievable as all of this information was to Chemah, he had to finally admit that it was the only feasible explanation. He had indeed noticed the captain's eyes while fighting him. He had seen those eyes before in the derelict at Popeyes and in other strangers who passed him on the street. At the time, he thought he was delusional due to sleep deprivation. He had, after all, been existing on only a couple of hours of sleep a day since Héro was kidnapped.

Michelle stood outside the door listening. It all seemed so surreal to her: supervillains, soul transferring, it was too much to grasp.

Without turning around Lydia called to her.

"Come in, Michelle. Chemah needs jou now."

Chemah looked toward the door and tears came to his eyes as Michelle entered.

The sight of Chemah crying brought sympathetic tears to Michelle's eyes. She entered the room slowly and cautiously, using her reflexes and other senses to guide her around the room's contents, just as she'd done many times before. Only this time, she was blinded by the sight of the most beautiful man that she had ever seen. She wiped the tears from her eyes loathing the small droplets for obscuring her view of Chemah for even a moment. The light that radiated around Chemah made the bed he lay in look like a deified shrine. Michelle moved slowly toward the bed, scared to take her eyes off of Chemah lest her vision should leave her again and she would only have the fleeting memory of his piercing gray eyes forcing their way through hers to caress her soul. Michelle reached the side of the bed and Chemah reached out to touch her. Michelle's body shook from head to toe as Chemah's fingertips found the edges of her high cheekbones.

"I was worried about you."

Michelle closed her eyes and breathed deeply. The sound of his voice and his scent made her feel safe again. She could not find the power of her vocal cords to answer him and Chemah became concerned.

"What's wrong, baby?"

Michelle would not allow the tears to come again. She refused to be deprived of any sight of Chemah. She reached out to touch his face and felt the power in him course through her. It was electric, the way it had been the first time they met, but now their wireless connection was complete. She welcomed his soul through her eyes and they embraced each other's essence. Chemah's eyes pulled her body into his and she threw herself on top of him nearly pulling the IV out of his arm. When Lydia turned toward the bed one last time before leaving, Michelle's and Chemah's bodies were crushed and convulsing against each other as they mashed the other's lips and tore at each other's clothes.

Lydia closed the door behind her and stood guard outside. She still had more to say to him, but this was not the time.

The next morning the investigators came to interview Chemah. He was told the coroners announced that Captain Brea died of a heart attack brought on spontaneously by his late-stage brain cancer. Chemah only confirmed that the captain had been delusional when he came to Chemah's home and attacked him. Chemah had nothing to gain by telling the Internal Affairs investigators what truly transpired. He was, after all, still looking forward to a long career with the department.

Chapter 25

Journey to the Beginning

Three weeks after what everyone was calling "the incident," Chemah was getting dressed for his first day as a newly promoted lieutenant. It was the department's way of trying to sweep away the fact that one of their high-ranking officers tried to kill their best detective. Fortunately the story never made the newspapers and Chemah took the promotion without any undo celebrating.

Chemah knew it would be his last promotion for a long time. It wasn't that he couldn't make captain in another three or four years, but lieutenant was the highest rank that he could have and still be on the streets making collars and solving crimes. He would have to supervise other detectives, but at least he would not be relegated to a desk for the rest of his career. He knew he was meant to save lives and help the poor and innocent. The other morning Tatsuya told him he wanted to be a policeman like him, and he remembered that he was approximately Tatsuya's age when he decided that he wanted to help people who were in trouble.

Chemah was tying the shoelace of his right oxford when he heard a commotion downstairs. It was the voices of two women arguing.

Michelle came out of the bathroom with her hair still in a dooby.

"What the hell is going on downstairs? Is Lydia here already?"

Chemah jumped from the side of the bed and blocked Michelle's path before she could make it to the door. He grabbed her by the waist and pulled her close to him, kissing her gently on the lips and then holding and biting her lower lip, making her laugh and cry out.

"Ooh, ooh, didn't you get enough last night?" Michelle tried to pull away from his hungry mouth, but kept her arms laced around his neck.

"Do you think I could ever get enough of you?" Chemah breathed into her mouth.

Michelle felt her heart pounding again as he breathed his desire into her with his words. Her heart raced as it always did when he spoke to her in this manner and she gave herself to him again as easily as she had last night. Before she realized it, she was on her tiptoes, his zipper was open, and he entered her without any struggle. They stood motionless five feet from the open doorway of their bedroom, communicating their eternal love through the ardor in their eyes. Only the grinding of their hips gave them away as they appeared to be a single statue of lovers standing against time. Michelle's breath came in gasps as she felt the hardness of Chemah's throbbing flesh spasm continuously inside of her. Chemah broke the spell of their unspoken love with a tender kiss on her neck.

"Daddy, Daddy, Mama's here and Miss Lydia won't let her in the house!"

"Oh, fuck." Chemah greedily thrust into Michelle one last time, making her stand painfully on the very tips of her toes for an agonizing second, before extracting himself from Michelle in a heated rush. Chemah ran into the bathroom to conceal his erection a second before his daughter came running through the open door.

Michelle was still breathless and panting a little and it seemed easier to bend a knee to listen to the girl at her height.

"Hurry up! Mama's at the door and Miss Lydia said she'll beat her if she sets one foot inside!"

"Michelle, can you handle that? I'm having a little trouble putting some stuff away right now."

Michelle laughed at his plight, but as she heard the commotion downstairs she thought better than to tease him. Those two women were dangerous and there was no telling who would win that fight.

"I'll take care of your business downstairs. You keep a hand on things up here." She giggled as Héro grabbed her hand and pulled her through the doorway.

When they reached the bottom of the stairs the sight that greeted Michelle and Héro was almost comical. Miss Lydia had a long knife in one hand and was holding Base by his collar with the other. Margarita was flat against the front door leading into the living room, and she was spewing curses at the elder woman. When she saw Michelle, she cried out for her help.

"Will you tell this crazy old bitch to put that knife down and call this damn dog off?"

"I'm crazy? No, jou are crazy! Jou think jou can yust walk into this house like it is jours."

Margarita almost came off the door to strike Lydia at her suggestion that the house she helped renovate with her own hands was not rightfully hers. A quick snap from Base's jowls at her extended right hand changed her mind.

Days after "the incident," Chemah had asked around and finally found Lydia at her store on One Hundred Sixteenth Street. She was cleaning the storefront window under the sign that read *BOTANICA* when Chemah entered the store. Chemah finally recognized Lydia as the beautiful woman who had kissed him on the forehead when he was a little boy those many years ago when he first passed this same store.

Chemah thanked Lydia over and over again for finding Héro and returning her to him. Tatsuya told him how he and Miss Lydia met on the street the day that he took Base for a walk. Tatsuya brazenly lied saying that Base led them to a building where Miss Lydia went inside and found Héro. As much as Chemah had questioned him, Tatsuya would not change his story. Later the FBI came to the house to follow up on the solved case and they couldn't get any more out of Tatsuya than Chemah had. Chemah gave them Lydia's name and they said they would follow up.

"The FBI came to see you?

"They came. They had some questions and they were satisfied with my answers."

Chemah raised an eyebrow at her haughtiness.

"I have helped them on occasion, jou know. Do jou know Director McNeil?"

Chemah knew of the director of the FBI in New York, but did not know him personally.

"I told those men who came in their black suits to call him. I gave them his number. He told them I was okay and they left."

Her story was unbelievable, but Chemah left well enough alone. He offered Miss Lydia the reward money and to his relief she turned it down.

"It was the dog who found the baby. Didn't Tatsuya tell jou?"

"Yes, he told me and he also told me that Anthony Pone also helped you. Do you know where I can find him?"

"I could tell jou, but if jou found him he would probably want the reward."

"He is entitled."

"I know, I will tell him if I see him." The sarcastic look on Lydia's face was a clue that Chemah shouldn't push the subject. There was only one thing left for Chemah to say.

"If there is anything else I can ever do for you, all you have to do is ask."

That's how Lydia started working as the children's caregiver. She explained to Chemah how she intended to close the store as business had been waning after so many years in the now gentrified neighborhood. Lydia now needed gainful employment. She was willing to do housekeeping and care for the children and she lived close enough to Chemah that she could be there at a moment's notice.

Chemah went home and discussed it with Michelle, whereupon Michelle told him that she was seriously considering going on tour soon and he would need someone to care for the kids.

Funny how things worked out, Michelle thought as she stepped between the two women staring each other down in her living room.

"Lydia, please put that knife away and let Base go back into the yard."

"I'll go back into the kitchen. My *asopao de camaron,* shrimp soup, is almost finished, but I told the dog he could stay in the house with me today," she said, defying Michelle. Lydia made a production of backing away from Margarita without turning her back to her. Michelle was amazed at how Base backed away with Lydia barely jerking his collar.

At first sight of Lydia two weeks ago Michelle was skeptical about even letting her in the house. It wasn't until the children came from the backyard with Base and he sat at Lydia's feet without so much as a growl that Michelle knew for certain that Lydia must be a good person. Base didn't like anybody. He had even tried to bite Chemah when they first met. Recently she had even been a little jealous of Lydia and Base's relationship as Base seemed to prefer Lydia's company to hers when she was in the house. Since Michelle didn't need Base as a seeing-eye dog anymore, she rarely took him with her outside the house. Michelle loved that dog more than anything, even as much as she loved Chemah and the children, so she was glad that he had a new friend who would spend time with him.

"Sit down, Margarita. Chemah will be coming down in a minute. He had to take care of something upstairs."

Héro, who had been quietly standing next to Michelle the whole time, took Margarita's hand and led her toward the couch.

"I really didn't mean to intrude, Michelle. Chemah told me you would be leaving to go on tour this morning and I thought I would pick Héro up early and say good-bye to you."

Margarita looked in the direction of the kitchen and glared at the door.

"I didn't think I would be treated like some kind of murd—I mean, stranger."

Héro snuggled up next to her mother and Margarita's face softened as she put her arm around the little girl.

Michelle looked at the mother and daughter together and thought about the relationship that she shared with her own mother. She was glad that Margarita was trying so hard to be in Héro's life. As much as she loved the little girl, she was afraid that she would never be able to care for Héro in the way that her mother would.

Now that Michelle knew that she would be gone from the kids and Chemah for three months, she couldn't wait for the tour to start and finish so that she could come back home. After long hours of passion the night after she told Chemah she was going on tour, they finally set a date for their wedding. Two weeks from the day she got back from the tour, she would officially be Mrs. Michelle Rivers. That night they talked about having at least one more child and the next day she stopped taking birth control pills. She wanted her body to detox from the pill to be certain she would have no problems conceiving when she got back. Chemah even suggested that he would take the children on a two-week holiday to Europe while she was there. They wouldn't miss her so much, and they could start working on their new addition to the family. Thinking about all the things that she had never dared to dream about when she was blind made Michelle able to see the beauty in everything around her. She even dared to think she could look past Margarita's outer beauty to see the caring and thoughtfulness that Margarita had for the people she cared about. She always asked about Tatsuya's welfare, though Tatsuya refused to be anywhere within eyesight of her. And Michelle believed that if Chemah were in any kind of trouble, even if it were only for the sake of Héro, Margarita would be there for him. It was this thought that allowed Michelle to sit with Margarita for a full thirty minutes making small talk before she realized that it was almost time for her to go.

The doorbell rang and Michelle answered it. It was the driver who was to take her to the airport. After a brief introduction the driver asked Michelle if she had any luggage and Michelle pointed to the three Louis Vuitton suitcases that were neatly stacked at the bottom of the staircase. The driver was able to pick up all three bags at one time and Michelle held the door open for him.

"I'll be waiting in the car, ma'am. You don't have to rush. We have plenty of time to make it to the airport."

Michelle said *thank you* and made a mental note to give the man a big tip when he dropped her off. She turned back to Margarita and Héro who had risen from the couch. Margarita was straightening Héro's dress.

"I guess it's time for me to go."

Margarita got up from one knee and took Héro's hand.

"I guess it's time for us to be going, too."

Michelle walked to the staircase and shouted at the top of her lungs. "*Chemaaah, the car's here. Come down.*"

Margarita wrinkled her face up at the sound of Michelle's scream, but Michelle's back was to her and she did not see it.

Both women looked up the stairs expectantly as they heard Chemah's footsteps make their way down. It got so quiet when he came into view that you could have heard a mouse shitting in the woods.

Chemah rubbed the top of his smooth head.

"So what do you think?"

Héro spoke first.

"You're a baldy, Daddy."

Chemah laughed and looked at Michelle hopefully as he came to the last step.

"Baby, you look beautiful," Michelle said, coming to him and putting her arms around his neck. She kissed him hard on the lips and took the opportunity to thoroughly massage his scalp.

"Mmmmmm, that feels nice," Michelle said, breaking their kiss.

"What the hell did you do that for?"

Chemah and Michelle had forgotten that Margarita was still there and they both turned to her, their distaste for her comment obvious on their faces. Margarita felt their ire and retreated a little.

"I mean, that's a little drastic, isn't it?"

For the sake of his daughter, Chemah tried to keep the malice out of his voice and turned to explain to Michelle, instead of dignifying Margarita's remark.

"I thought I'd take it all off and start it again. New beginnings and all that, you know."

Michelle kissed him again and Margarita's remark was forgotten.

Lydia came bustling through the kitchen door. She was still holding Base by the collar, but he didn't seem to mind. She took one look at Chemah and beamed with pride as if he were her own son.

"Oh my Godyy! I told jou, jou would still be very handsome when the locks are cut off." Lydia turned and explained to Michelle. "The hair is like antennas, it draws good energy to it and bad energy too. It's better that he starts over now."

Chemah looked sheepish. He didn't want Michelle to know that he had cut his hair on the advice of this eccentric new friend.

"*Mijo,* did you save the locks for me like I told you to?"

"They're upstairs on the bathroom sink," Chemah said, still a little embarrassed that he was following Lydia's instruction.

"You're going to burn them, aren't you?" Michelle said, excited that she might know some secret voodoo mojo. "When my grandmother came to visit from the island she used to always burn any extra hair that was left on our combs and brushes."

"Yes, I have to burn the hair. Jou yest never know what someone will do with the power in it." Lydia turned accusingly toward Margarita, who took the hint.

"Alright. I'm leaving. Baby, say good-bye to your father and Michelle."

Héro kissed and hugged everyone good-bye. She already knew that Tatsuya wouldn't come down. He would wave good-bye to her from his bedroom window as was their ritual. Héro reached for her mother's hand again and Base made a lunge toward it again. Margarita took pleasure in seeing her daughter scold and hit the dog on the snout with her bare hand.

"Bad, Base, bad!"

Base lowered his head in shame at the admonishment and the other three adults felt sorry for the canine. Margarita's derisive smile was not lost on any of them.

"Have a good trip, dear." Margarita said to Michelle. She held the door open for Héro as the little girl waved a final time from the doorway.

"My car is waiting, baby. I don't want to miss my flight."

"Do you have everything?"

Michelle reached for Chemah and he took her in his arms for the last time.

"Now I have everything."

"Tatsuyaaah, come down and say good-bye!!" Lydia's voice was even louder than Michelle's.

Tatsuya came bounding down the stairs and jumped into Michelle's arms. Michelle struggled, but she was strong enough to hold the eleven-year-old boy. After a fierce hug that threatened to snap Michelle's back, Chemah finally interfered.

"Alright, that's enough now. We don't want her to be late."

Tatsuya reluctantly let go and ran back up the stairs without saying anything else. Chemah looked up after him and was about to remark on Tatsuya's quirkiness when Lydia spoke.

"Leave the boy alone. He's yust doing what comes natural to him. He's growing up."

Chemah couldn't dispute the obvious. Instead he took Michelle by the hand and walked her out to the waiting black car.

Lydia waited for Chemah at the top of the front steps and watched as

Chemah kissed his bride-*not*-to-be good-bye. Lydia knew that Michelle would not be returning from this trip. It had been foretold to her in a reading of the little girl's fortune. There was nothing that Lydia could do but stand by and watch the balance of good and bad tip to and fro. Once in a while she would be able to put powers into play that would put things in order, but for the most part she recognized herself as a pawn and did the bidding of nature, the universe, God, or any other name that anyone tried to give to the all-encompassing life force. There were rules to adhere to and she was their keeper.

Chemah waved a last time to the black car that headed down the street. The darkened rear window kept him from knowing if Michelle was waving back. He walked slowly back up the walkway and met Lydia at the top of the stairs. She was smiling at him with that twisted smile that he now recognized as chagrin and he decided that she was hiding something.

"Is there something that you want to tell me?"

"Me tell jou something? What can I tell jou? I don't know much."

"Mmm-hmm, yeah, you don't know much."

Chemah decided whatever it was she knew he might not want to know. He headed for the door, but Lydia stopped him with a question.

"Chemah, have you ever read *The Alchemist?*"

Chemah turned back to her.

"No, no, I don't think I have."

"It is a very good book. It was written by a man, I think his name was Paulo Coelho. He was a very smart man. In this book, he said, '*If it happens once it will probably never happen again. But if it happens twice, then it will definitely happen a third time.*'"

Chemah searched Lydia's eyes for some clue to her riddle, but could not read anything in her coal-black eyes.

"Agghh, I'm just a crazy old lady. Let's go inside and get some ice cream."

Chemah followed her inside, thinking the old lady had read his mind.

About the Author

David Rivera, Jr. has been writing short stories for many years and has been inspired by the writings of the contemporary black male writers who have emerged during the past few years. His first book, *Harlem's Dragon,* was received with great enthusiasm by other writers as well as literary critics. David lives in Harlem, U.S.A. with his family and aspires to reignite the literary flame that Harlem had been renowned for with his novels *Harlem's Dragon, The Street Sweeper,* and now *Playing in the Dark.* He received a bachelor's degree in sociology and a master's degree in public administration. David Rivera, Jr. can be contacted at setodavid@aol.com. Visit his web site at www.davidriverajr.com.

IF YOU ENJOYED "PLAYING IN THE DARK," GET STARTED ON THE BACK STORY WITH THIS EXCERPT FROM

Harlem's Dragon

THE LOVE YOU CAN'T FIGHT

David Rivera, Jr.

Chapter 5

Who stole the cookie from the cookie jar?

"Two-Ninety Central Park West," Chemah announced. "Last stop." He and Nairobi were still making silly jokes with each other.

"Would you like to come upstairs?" Nairobi asked, her face turning serious again. Chemah wanted to say yes, but tried to play it cool again. "I'll never find a parking space out here, I'd better just go," he said.

"Is it because I'm white?" she asked plainly.

"Because you're white?" Chemah repeated.

"Yeah, because I'm white, you think we shouldn't be together," Nairobi said genuinely.

"I never even thought about the color situation, Nairobi," Chemah said honestly. "I just move cautiously whenever I deal with women. We just met an hour ago and I thought maybe we were moving too fast."

"Too fast for what?" she snapped.

"Too fast to get to know each other better. Too fast for two people that obviously have chemistry to have a glass of wine?"

"Listen, Chemah, I keep my life very simple. If I don't like you, I stay away from you. If I like you, then I want you around me. Life is too short, and I plan to enjoy every minute that I can. I know you like me, so stop fronting."

Chemah laughed at her attempt to use slang.

"Yes, stop fronting," she repeated.

"Nairobi, are you trying to say frontin'?"

"That's what I said," she repeated, "fronting."

Chemah laughed again. "Your ebonics are terrible," he said. "Who's been teaching you this awful slang?"

"My students teach me sometimes," she said proudly.

"Then by all means...We had better spend more time together, you really ought to practice more. Your pronunciation is deplorable." They both laughed.

"I'll tell you what," she said. "You go around the block a few times, and look for a parking spot; that'll give me some time to tidy the place up. I wasn't expecting any company, and I left the place a mess this morning."

"OK," Chemah said this time. "I'll bring your box upstairs."

"I'll let the doorman know I'm expecting you. Don't take too long."

"What apartment?" Chemah screamed after her.

"Fifteen A," she called over her shoulder.

Twenty minutes later Chemah was in the elevator on his way up to Nairobi's apartment. The doorman had been expecting him and attempted to take the box from his arms. "Thank you. I'll take it up myself," he assured him.

"Yes, sir," the doorman said, being accommodating.

Chemah looked up and down the hall as he stepped off the elevator and stood in the middle of the hall. He saw the apartment number 15A approximately ten feet away to his left. He walked to the door, but as he reached to touch the doorbell, the door swung inward.

Nairobi stood at the threshold to the door and smiled. "Come in, the coast is clear." She had changed her clothes. She wore gray sweat pants and a T-shirt. Chemah looked at her from head to toe and saw that she was barefoot. Her feet were well pedicured. Chemah and his friends always discussed how important it was for a woman to have nice feet. Chemah crossed the doorway and walked down a hallway littered with pictures on the wall. Chemah noticed that Nairobi was in most of the pictures; the other people he guessed were family members. The living room was immense. It housed two huge bookcases opposite each other; they ran wall to wall, and floor to ceiling. Neither one looked as if it could house another book.

"Make yourself comfortable," Nairobi said. "I'll get us some wine."

Chemah sat on a couch that he thought he had seen in an IKEA catalog, and Nairobi came into the living room with two glasses of wine. "You haven't read all of these books, have you?" he asked.

"No, I inherited them from my family," she said as she handed Chemah a glass and sat close to him. "Ninety-five percent of them were already here when I got here."

"So this is your family's apartment?" he asked.

"No, it's my apartment. It used to belong to my grandmother, and she put me on the lease. When she died I took it over. It's rent stabilized so they can't raise the rent any more than when my grandmother was alive. She and my grandfather lived here for over fifty years. On a teacher's salary that's the only way I can afford to live on Central Park West."

"I was going to ask you how you could afford to live here, but I thought it would be rude," Chemah said.

"You'd be surprised how many people inherit their apartments from parents and grandparents out here. I know some families who damn near go to war over who gets their grandparents' apartment."

A silence subtly settled between Nairobi and Chemah as they looked at each other. Nairobi inched closer to him. "Chemah, can I be totally honest with you?" Chemah nodded yes not knowing what she would say next. She began, "Like I told you in the car, when I meet someone whose vibe is on an even keel with mine, I make it my business to spend time with them. I don't want this to come out sounding like some line that I give every man I meet because I really don't. I mean I haven't been in a relationship in a long time. What I'm trying to say is I find myself very attracted to you. I feel a warmth from you that I don't normally feel from anyone when I first meet them. I'm not trying to scare you; I know we just met one hour ago, but I believe in love at first sight."

Chemah was startled by what she said, but he kept his composure. "I'm feeling you too, Nairobi; I just don't know if it's love right now." In actuality, Chemah knew it was love the moment she got into his car. He was fighting it with every bit of his mother's anti-white rationale. She had told him on more than one occasion, there's only one thing a white woman wants a black man for. Nairobi took his hand in hers. He could feel the softness and firmness of them.

"I'm not telling you my feelings to obligate you, Chemah," she said. "I just felt that some part of you was not allowing you to pursue me; and I just wanted you to know that I'm yours if you want me."

"Just like that, if I want you I can have you?" Chemah felt a wave of pleasure wash over him like the first time he'd held a girl's hand. He felt those unusual butterflies he got when he was twelve years old and he'd first told a girl he loved her. His mother had called it puppy love. "Nairobi, I haven't even kissed you yet."

"If you kiss me do you think it will change the way, you feel about me?"

"I don't know."

"Then kiss me and find out."

"That won't prove anything," he said. "How can you know in so short a period of time that you're in love in with someone?"

Nairobi leaned back, and away from him putting her hand behind the couch for support. "I know because I've been waiting to feel like this for a long time. I've never felt it before so it must be love," she answered.

Chemah thought he'd throw her a curve ball when he asked, "How many Black men have you been with?" It was always a possibility that she just had jungle fever.

"I've never been with a Black man," she said matter-of-factly. "Chemah, maybe I've taken the wrong approach. Why don't we just relax and drink our wine, and you can tell me more about yourself." This line of conversation was easier for him to get into, but immediately left him wanting that feeling he felt when she was expressing her feelings for him.

Chemah started by telling her he was one of three sons; the middle child. He told her his educational background, and how he had gone about getting a master's degree in forensic science and his job in a forensics lab. He even told her of his aspirations to work for the NYPD. They traded stories most of the evening; not thinking or even feeling the need for sustenance other than each other's company. When Chemah finally looked at his watch it was one-fifteen a.m. "I think it might be time for me to go," he said reluctantly.

"What time is it?"

"One-fifteen a.m."

"You could spend the night if you want. No strings attached."

"You know that's the same line I used on girls in college."

"It's not a line; you can sleep on the couch if you'd like. I just want to know that you're near me." The butterflies in his stomach were coming back; he was really feeling her now.

"Which way is the bedroom?" Chemah asked as he stood. Nairobi took his hand in hers and guided him down another hall to her bedroom. The bedroom was almost as big as her living room. Its space was not minimized by the few items she had in it: a king-sized bed with matching Ralph Lauren sheets and comforter (he had the same ones on his bed); a massage table next to the window facing the park; and a desk with a computer in the corner. The place was so immaculate it seemed she didn't use the room at all.

"We may have one problem," Chemah said. "I sleep in the nude."

"It's not a problem for me if it's not a problem for you. I sleep in the nude, too," she said.

"Are you trying to make me think that the two of us are going to be nude in this bed and nothing is going to happen?"

"I didn't say nothing was going to happen. No strings attached."

She shrugged her shoulders and pulled at his belt. Chemah took this as a cue that they would be undressing each other. He reached for the string on her sweatpants, but was intercepted by Nairobi's swift moving hands. She pushed his hands back to his sides, and as he was about to object, she put her index finger to his lips signaling for him to be quiet. Nairobi's eyes never lost contact with his as his pants fell to his ankles. Nairobi held his hips briefly and began lowering herself using first his hips, then his thighs to steady herself as she slowly descended to her knees. Chemah almost broke his silence to tell her that he didn't wear underwear but thought maybe she'd already figured it out. As she reached eye level with his penis, she broke eye contact with his eyes and stared admiringly at what he had to offer.

Chemah's excitement was becoming obvious; he started to thicken and lengthen right in front of her face, but all she did was stare. After a few moments of staring at his privates, her eyes and hands went to his feet. Undoing the bow in his laces she helped him take his shoes and socks off one after the other. She was then able to gently remove the remainder of his pants from around his ankles. Nairobi got off her knees with no help from him, and walked to the massage table neatly placing the pants on the table and the shoes and socks under it. Chemah felt silly standing there with nothing on but his Coogi sweater, so he pulled it off before she could turn back to him.

Nairobi turned toward him again and pouted as he extended his hand to her with the sweater in it. "I wanted to take that off you," she said. "I've been thinking about it since I first saw you this afternoon."

"So it's just been my body all along?"

"Noooo, it's just that you're so beautiful I wanted to unveil all of you myself," she replied.

"Well, when do I get to unveil you?"

"You don't," Nairobi said as she reached the wall and turned out the lights.

"I don't, huh," Chemah said, reaching for her in the dark, and missing. As his eyes adjusted to the darkness, he could make out Nairobi slipping into bed and out of his reach. Chemah carefully made his way to the bed and found his way under the sheets next to Nairobi. He felt for some part of Nairobi's body in the huge king-size bed, and found her hand. Chemah squeezed it gently and simultaneously pulled her to him as he pushed his body forward to meet hers.

His eyes had fully adjusted to the darkness and he could see Nairobi's face by the moonlight coming through the window.

Chemah bent to kiss her and as their lips touched, her tongue entered his mouth searching for something soft and moist. Their tongues slipped in and out of each other's mouths as their kissing became more and more frantic. When he thought he couldn't take it anymore, he reached for the string on her sweat pants and pulled it. Her pants were immediately loose and he slipped his hand inside to touch her. Nairobi was very wet. Chemah easily entered her with a finger. Nairobi detached herself from his mouth and began kissing his neck as her breathing came harshly through clenched teeth. Chemah needed to gain more leverage to stimulate her with his hand, so he stopped touching her and used that same hand to tug her sweats off. As she felt him tugging, she lifted her hips off the mattress, and in one swift motion the pants were around her ankles. She kicked them off quickly; and he used that moment to tug her T-shirt over her head. Nairobi manipulated his penis in a jerky motion with her hand, as he kissed and licked her breast. Chemah slid his hand down her stomach to touch the moistness again. She caught his hand and guided it lower than he had intended to go.

"Get me ready, here," she said breathily, slipping his middle finger into her ass. Chemah had heard that some women preferred anal sex to vaginal sex, but he would have never guessed that Nairobi was one of those women. Either way as hard as she had gotten him, he wasn't going to argue. Chemah didn't know where she pulled it from, but he heard the tearing sound of a condom wrapper and the *thppt* sound you make spitting the remaining rapper from your mouth. Nairobi worked hard to put the condom over his penis as he continued to lave her breast and pump his finger into her ass using the vaginal juices that dripped out of her as a lubricant. Nairobi let him know she was ready to be entered by pulling him on top of her. Using his erection as a leash, she guided him to the space she wanted him to enter and pulled her legs far back so that her knees were against her shoulders.

Chemah had never had anal intercourse before, but like all men he fantasized about it many times. Initially, he was careful as he entered her, pulling back slowly, and entering her slowly again. Nairobi urged, "Do it harder, Chemah. Faster, faster. Oh God, make love to me." She grabbed a handful of his buttocks and pulled him into her. This kind of sex was everything he had imagined it to be. Raw and animalistic. Chemah came twice without ever getting soft or leaving her body. After the second time, he pulled out of her. Chemah was still rock hard. He knew it was the excitement of having fulfilled a fantasy and the newness of the relationship that was keeping him hard.

Chemah lay on his back trying to catch his breath. "Are you alright?" Nairobi asked, kissing his chest.

"Yeah, just give me a second to catch my breath, then you can show me to the shower."

"You're still hard," Nairobi noticed out loud.

"After I get out of the shower, we can make love again if you're not too tired."

"No, honey, I'm not tired; we can do it as many times as you like," Nairobi responded. She led him to the bathroom. He took a quick shower and came out ready to go again. This time he intended to make her come as fast as she had made him come. Chemah walked into the bedroom again and Nairobi was standing at the window staring out into the park. The room was still dark but he could see her silhouette against the light outside. She was still naked and looked beautiful. She had pulled her hair back so you could see her entire face.

Chemah came up behind her encircling her in his arms. "Hmmmm," she murmured, "that feels good," as he pressed his hardening penis against her backside. He turned her around to face him and saw tears forming in her eyes.

"What's wrong?" he asked. "Did I do something to hurt you?"

"No. You've been perfect from the moment I met you."

"Then why are you crying?" Chemah asked, not understanding her pain.

"Because I'm happy and I never want it to end."

"It doesn't have to end," Chemah said, lifting her into his arms and carrying her to the bed. This time he meant to make love to her slowly letting her know that his feelings for her were also very strong. They kissed each other ardently. Each touching and feeling the other with the intensity that is born with finding your soul mate.

"I'm a virgin," Nairobi said, unexpectedly breaking their kiss.

"Huh, what was that?" Chemah said stupidly.

"I AM A VIRGIN," Nairobi said, exaggerating each word.

Chemah stared at Nairobi through the darkness. "What are you talking about? We just got busy twenty minutes ago."

"We just had anal sex twenty minutes ago," she corrected him. "I've never been vaginally penetrated."

Chemah lay staring at her for a moment and then asked her the only question that came to his head. "Why?"

"Why am I a virgin or why do I have anal sex, or is your question why am I telling you now?" she said vehemently.

Chemah kept his composure. "Why don't you just tell me everything you want me to know on the subject of your virginity? If I have any questions when you finish I'll let you know."

"Well, it's very simple actually," Nairobi said. "My mother always told me that I should save my virginity for a special person. That person would be my husband. My mother's advice to me on my first date was that a boy would do anything he could to stick his penis into my vagina; so I should do everything that I could to not allow that to happen.

"My first date was John Delaney—blond hair, blue eyes, and a smile that broke through all my defenses," she continued. "I told John that I was saving my virginity for someone special, and John convinced me after a time that you didn't have to have vaginal sex to have fun. Sitting in my parents' living room watching TV after midnight on a Saturday, John and I started petting after my parents went to bed. John and my teenage insecurities convinced me that anal sex was okay. After all, Mom never said I shouldn't do it. Anyway he was the first, I enjoyed it, and all my other boyfriends since haven't complained when I offered them my buttocks in place of my vagina. I've since learned that almost all men fantasize about what I have always thought of as the natural thing to do. Including you," she said slyly.

"What do you mean, including me?" Chemah said, sitting up in her bed.

"Are you trying to say, you didn't enjoy the sex we just had?" Nairobi asked.

"I'm not saying I didn't enjoy it; I'm just saying that it's not my main concern when I'm having sex with a woman."

"And what is your main concern, Mr. Rivers?" Nairobi asked, reaching for his hand in the dark. Chemah was not ready to let Nairobi know all of his secrets yet. The white girl had him open, and she knew it. Chemah had to close the gap a little.

"I'm concerned about getting some sleep," he said, lying down and turning his back to her. Chemah could feel Nairobi smiling in the dark as she laid her arm over his body and ticked herself into the small of his back in spoon fashion. She softly kissed the back of his neck, and gave him one last squeeze before whispering a soft "good night" into his ear. He never fell asleep feeling that secure again.

Chemah awoke slowly feeling that he was still in the dream that he had just been disturbed from. He felt a soft moistness on his dick that was all too familiar. Raising himself onto his elbows he questioned the darkness. "What are you—" he started.

Nairobi continued to raise his nature with her mouth, but she gently urged him onto his back using her soft hands to put pressure on his chest. Her mouth never skipped a beat. Chemah could see through the window that the sun was starting to rise. The sky was a light purple, but it enabled him to see clearly in its glow. He looked down at Nairobi and saw that she was staring back at him. Her eyes dared him to try and hold back another orgasm. As his hips involuntarily began to jerk upward to meet Nairobi's mouth earnestly, she suddenly released him from her grip. The cool dawn air against his wet penis was uncomfortable enough to stop his orgasm. Chemah wasn't about to beg her to make him come, and he didn't have to. Nairobi kissed her way up his leg and on to his stomach, where she lingered to tongue his belly button. As she kissed her way up to his chest and then his neck, she simultaneously grabbed his dick. Chemah could feel the entrance to Nairobi's vagina dripping onto his hardness as she attempted to nestle the tip into her opening.

Chemah wanted to tell her she didn't have to do this. He wanted to tell her to save her virginity for someone who deserves her, but the only thing to come from his mouth was a breathless, "yessss." Chemah was in her raw dog (no condom, no contraceptives). It had been years since he made love to a woman without a condom, and the sensation that a woman's gripping vagina gives a man when it's skin to skin, almost made him weep.

He was concentrating on not cumming almost immediately after he was in her. She had already given him two orgasms and he didn't want to cum again until she got a few in herself. Whenever he felt himself about to blow, he would forcefully stop the thrust of her hips with his hands and go into a slower stroke that he could control. Chemah thought she had come as soon as she had impaled herself on him. She was shuddering and shaking as if she was having an epileptic attack, but he figured that was impossible. No woman comes that fast. They were both slippery with sweat and he couldn't hold it back any longer. Chemah felt his balls were about to crack open, they were so ready. "I can't hold it," he gasped.

"Give it to me, Chemah. Give me all of you. I'm cumming," Nairobi exalted. Chemah's cum blasted through him and into her when she made that announcement. They clung to one another, each riding out the other's orgasm. "Are you alright?" Nairobi asked as they lay holding each other.

"Shouldn't I be asking you that question?"

Nairobi smiled. "I'm happy."

"You're not in any pain, are you?"

"Shouldn't you have asked me that question two hours ago?" she said, raising her eyebrows.

"I'm sorry."

She one-upped him. "I love you." They both drifted to sleep lazily lying in each other's arms.